# DRAGON'S DREAM

Tom R. Lupara

Order this book online at www.trafford.com
or email orders@trafford.com

Most Trafford titles are also available at major online book retailers.

Printed in the United States of America.

ISBN: 978-1-4669-6654-3 (sc)
ISBN: 978-1-4669-6653-6 (e)

Trafford rev. 12/29/2012

 www.trafford.com

North America & international
toll-free: 1 888 232 4444 (USA & Canada)
phone: 250 383 6864 ♦ fax: 812 355 4082

DRAGON'S DREAM
by Tom R. Lupara


The dark clouds churn ominously above the green Scottish

countryside with the distant roll of thunder. Moments later fresh

drops of rain patter the wind-blown grass and ripple the steeled

surface of the distant lake, the rich musk of damp soil rising

from the earth. On the rocky hillside below a scatterd herd of

sheep bleat as they hurry away, heading for shelter from the

coming storm.

It was here, in this pristine land, that the fiercest of all

dragons once reigned supreme.

Known as Temper, this dragon was unlike any other the world

had ever known. His mighty wings could block out the sun when he

took to the sky. His flame was an inferno. The force of his jaws

could snap trees in two. His jade scales were impenetrable to the

weapons of his enemies. Because of this, many believed Temper not

to be a dragon at all, but rather a leviathan released from the
depths of hell to spread fear and spill the blood of the
innocent.

When Temper had first arrived in this land, king Warrington
had ordered his army to find and dispatch of this monster which
plagued his subjects. The brave band of soldiers had set out to
fulfill the king's orders, only to experience firsthand the
dragon's sheer ferocity.

On the battlefield Temper's flame had cooked whole advances
of knights within their armor. His mighty tail smashed the life
out of charging warriors. His jaws ripped soldiers in half, and
his fearsome horns skewered their steeds through the middle. The
battle had soon ended with Temper standing poised amongst a sea
of mangled and charred corpses, black smoke rising from his
nostrils, blood dripping off his plated scales, his reptilian red
eyes blazing with murderous triumph.

His army slaughtered, his lands held captive, king
Warrington had no other choice but to surrender his castle and
flee the land, abandoning his subjects to fend for themselves
against the fearsome dragon.

For the many long, dark years that followed, Temper ruled
these lands. At will he terrorized the peasants, feasting
on them and their livestock, snatching what meager riches they
possessed and forcing them to live in constant, cowering terror.
Those that attempted to flee his domain were slaughtered.

Then one day a Dragon Slayer came to this land, claiming the
ability to kill Temper with a strange new weapon the likes of

which none had ever before seen. Few believed it could be done, but after a harrowing battle the Dragon Slayer indeed bested Temper, toppling the beast from power and freeing the land from his rule. Saved from the dragon's torments, the peasants rejoyced with their new-found freedom, all believing Temper to have been killed by the brave Dragon Slayer.

They had been wrong.

Wounded, crippled, and defeated, yes, but dead Temper was most certainly not. Unbeknownst to them, Temper had continued to live on, once again proving himself incapable of dying at the hands of humans.

And it is here, in this drizzly stretch of land before us, that Temper continues to live on to this very day, fearfully hidden away from the very humans that had once cowered in his shadow.

Overhead the dark gray clouds churn as lightning flickers on the bleary horizon, the booming roll of thunder not far behind. The gentle patter of rain intensifies into a heavy downpour, dripping off the wind-shivered leaves of an oak tree and splashing in puddles amongst the lush green grass.

This rain water is absorbed by the rich soil, slowly drawn beneath ground. As it begins its gradual descent into the earth, the water passes through the fine layers of topsoil, past bits of rock and twisting roots. Deeper and deeper into the ground this water travels, seeping through thick layers of stratum, past large boulders, down past the reach of even the thickest roots and tunnels of burrowing rodents.

    After a time of this gradual descent, a single bead of water
squeezes through the sandstone roof of a subterranean cavern. The
bead of water snakes along the uneven surface of the stone,
slithering blindly on an unhurried course, before trickling down
the length of a stalactite. There the water pools at the
stalactite's inverted point, stretching downward like a single
tear before breaking away and falling into the darkness below.

    Plink.

    The bead of water splashes on Temper's scales muzzle as he
sleeps curled on the cold, hard stone floor of the subterranean
cavern.

    Once the fiercest dragon the world had ever known, Temper is
now but a shadow of the monster he'd once been. The sharp horns
which had once jutted menacingly from the top of his head are now
gone, replaced by two jagged, splintered stumps. His plated jade
scales are now brittle and dull, interrupted by massive puckered
scars marring his flanks. His once majestic wings are now
crippled and weak, as torn and withered as the sails of a ghost
ship.

    As he sleeps undisturbed by the water trickling down his
snout, Temper's scaled eyelids begin to twitch and spasm. His
mouth peels open in a snarl, revealing massive, dull yellow
teeth. A low growl rumbles from deep inside his massive body with
the power to shake the stalactites hanging from the cavern's
roof.

In his dream Temper is remembering the terrible might he
once possessed, and reliving the savage battle which stole it all
away...

CHAPTER 2

The red-hot sword blade hissed as Urick stabbed it into a
bucket of water, steam rising into his sweaty, grimy face. Urick
was a large man, his forearms thick with muscle earned from long
years of hard labor working as a blacksmith. His dark, sweaty
hair was pushed back off his brow, his leather apron streaked
with soot and scorch marks.

Once the steel cooled he pulled the sword out and held it
up, sliding a calloused hand down its length as he inspected the
blade with narrowed green eyes.

"Ready the coals. This edge is still too thick," he said
over his shoulder.

Across the cluttered, haze-filled workshop, Orion
immediately began manning the bellows, pushing bursts of air
across the flaring bed of red-hot coals with a rhythmic
hiss-wheeze.

Orion was Urick's son, a fact made evident by their striking resemblance to one another. Orion, a young man of seventeen, was a perfect reflexion of his father from twenty years past; his square, handsome face not yet lined with creases or made rough with a dark beard of stubble. His lean body was strong and capable, but lacking the hardened knots of muscle accumulated over many years of pounding iron.

Urick pushed the sword into the bed of hot coals, glowing red embers dancing up into the heat-shimmered air. "That blade will have to be hammered a while longer. You finish it. I'll start on William's bridle."

"Of course, father," Orion said as he continued to pump the bellows over the coals, sweat rolling in beads off his determined face.

Urick smiled, the faintest tug at the corners of his mouth and eyes as he walked over to a workbench and began to pound out a bridle with heavy clacks of his hammer. He no longer needed to tell Orion how to work iron--the young man had practically grown up beside a hot bed of coals. The family trade, Orion had learned from him just as Urick had from his own father: Long days spent side by side in the acrid heat of the smithy, pounding glowing rods of iron and losing gallons of sweat. In Urick's opinion, there was no better way to strengthen the bond between a father and son than hard labor. Words were few and rarely needed, only the combined will of two men working together to accomplish a job. There were much easier ways to earn a living, but just as

the iron they forged under heat and hammer, so a life of labor
forged a boy into a man.

"Damnit...!" Orion cursed under his breath from across the
workshop.

Hearing this, Urick stopped hammering and looked up to see
Orion shaking his hand, wincing. The boy had accidentally
scorched his hand on the hot metal--an unavoidable occurrence in
the smithy.

"Everything alright over there?" Urick asked with a frown.

"Fine, father. Fine," Orion said without looking back,
quickly picking up a pair of tongs to turn the sword in the
coals, trying to conceal that he'd burned himself.

Urick grinned, a full smile this time, and with a humorous
shake of his head resumed hammering the bridle. The boy was just
like him, never admitting to feeling pain no matter how badly it
hurt.

Meanwhile, outside the blacksmith's tent, Maribel was making
her way past a scattered group of villagers in the dirt lane
between huts. She was a beautiful young woman, with long dark
hair braided back to reveal her full, open face. She wore a plain
white dress, slightly tattered and stained around the hem, which
hardly concealed the fullness of her breasts nor the rounded
swell of her hips.

Waving the bitter smoke away from her face, Maribel arrived
at the blacksmith's tent and called out, "Father! Father, are you
busy in there?"

Urick set his hammer down on the workbench and smiled at his daughter. Pulling a dingy rag from his pocket he mopped the sweat from the back of his neck as he walked over to her. "Not at all, dear. What brings you here this time of day?" he asked, the hiss-wheeze of the bellows continuing as Orion heated the coals behind him.

Maribel smiled and held up a cloth-covered basket as if it were a surprise gift. "I brought you two lunch. Bread rolls, salt pork, and apples."

Urick fixed his daughter with a curious frown as he reached over the table and took the basket from her hands. "A special occasion?" he asked, folding back the cloth and smelling the salt pork.

Maribel tilted her head at her father as if slightly offended. "None whatsoever! I merely thought you two might be hungry, so I came to help. Can't I do so?"

Urick gave a conceding smile and folded the cloth back over the basket. "Of course, dear--anytime you wish. Thank you. It smells wonderful."

He was turning back to his workbench to finish molding the bridle when she added hastily, "Although, there is one little thing..."

Urick gave a wizened half-smile as he turned back. Orion may have taken after him, but Maribel was her mother through and through. "And what might that be?" he inquired, patiently setting the basket down and leaning his weight on his palms.

Maribel stalled for a moment, then blurted out all at once,

"Isabel's selling a round of blue cloth for two silver coins. Oh! You should see it, father. I could sew the loveliest dress. I'd look beautiful!"

"You're a beautiful girl already, Maribel. You don't need decoration."

"You're required to say that, father," Maribel countered. "Besides, how will I ever meet a worthy suitor wearing old rags such as these?" To emphasize her point, Maribel stepped back and motioned to her dress with an unflattering wave of her hands.

Urick forced himself to take a slow, patient breath before he replied. Maribel was at the age where girls began searching for husbands and preparing to leave home. It was the natural way. But no matter how much she grew, how many years passed by, Urick would always see her as his spunky little green-eyed girl. To hear her speak of suitors and marriage always thoroughly irritated him. He wasn't ready for her to grow up. Not quite yet, anyway.

Finally, Urick said, "I wasn't aware you had anyone in mind as a suitor."

Maribel looked at him with intense exasperation, as if shocked he'd said such a thing aloud for others to hear. "You know very well that I don't!" she said, sounding humorously offended. "And until I present myself properly, I doubt I ever will!"

Urick grunted and glanced away down the dirt street, thinking that wouldn't be such a terrible thing.

"Please, father?" Maribel asked, her beautiful face
pleading. "Please? Just two silver coins. I'd be so happy."

Urick put on his best show of reluctance while wiping his
dirty, stubbled neck with a soiled rag. He adored his daughter,
and she very much knew it, always using his affection to
manipulate his will as easily as a handfull of putty. Realizing
it was useless, he tucked the rag back into his pocket and said,
"I'll be expecting lunch all week." He turned and made his way
back into the workshop.

"Ah! Thank you, father!" Maribel called after him, smiling
happily.

While Maribel waited outside the blacksmith's tent for her
father to return with the coins, groups of villagers strolled
past on the hut-lined street behind her, busy attending their
daily chores.

One of those villagers happened to be a thin, dark-haired
young man who'd just parked his horse-drawn cart and was busy
unloading caged rabbits off the back. He was stacking them on the
roadside when Maribel, standing all alone across the street,
caught his eye. Distracted by the sight of her, he stacked one
last cage and straightened up, wiping his hands clean on the
front of his shirt as his dark eyes drifted unabashedly over her
body. He licked his thin lips.

After a moment the young man abandoned his cartload of
rabbits and began making his way across the street, hurriedly
brushing past villagers strolling by. When he came upon Maribel

her back was still turned, so he reached out a hand and tapped
her shoulder.

Startled, Maribel flinched and turned around. When she saw
who it was standing behind her she put her hand to her chest and
let out a quick, uncomfortable laugh. "Conner! Don't do that. You
frightened me," she said.

"Sorry," Conner apologized, smiling unctuously. His teeth
were ringed with plaque and looked much too small for his face,
as if he'd never lost his baby teeth. That combined with his
pale, angular features, knobby chin, and dark, middle-parted oily
hair gave him an unhealthily gaunt appearance.

"I didn't mean to frighten you. But I haven't seen you in
days...Where have you been, Maribel?" Conner inquired, stepping
closer.

Maribel took an immediate step back, trying to keep a
cushion of distance between them. "Oh...here and there," she
explained elusively. "I've been busy lately, you understand.
Sewing, cooking and cleaning--"

"Did you find the flower that I left for you?" Conner
interrupted, still grinning lecherously. He raised his dark
eyebrows in anticipation of her answer.

"Yes, the flower. About that...," Maribel recalled as she
glanced away, troubled by the memory.

For the last several months Conner had been doggedly
pursuing her. It had started out innocently enough, she supposed:
Him making up excuses for awkward conversation when they met in

the market; going out of his way to carry her things;

complementing her every dress. When that had failed to impress

her, Conner had taken a bolder approach: Frequently asking her

out on dates; inviting her on horse rides; offering her over to

his home for dinner. When even this proved ineffective, Conner's

attempts became even bolder and far more unsettling. He began

showing up in odd places at unexpected times, as if he'd been

waiting there for her to arrive. He became progressively more

confrontational and aggressive in his pursuit. His former

pleasantness began to wear thin, revealing his impatience and

anger whenever she failed to accept his advances.

Finding that she was beginning to feel frightened by his

presence, Maribel had recently been going out of her way to

avoid Conner, a futile effort which only seemed to attract him

all the more. Most recently, Maribel had awoken with a start in

the middle of the night to find a single rose placed on the

window ledge above her bed in her family's one room hut. When

she'd gotten out of bed and picked up the rose to investigate,

she'd seen a thin silhouette--Conner--slip away into the

darkness. That single gesture had sent goosebumps of alarm

prickling across her flesh, her every instinct screaming danger.

Of course, Maribel had decided against telling her father

any of this for fear of his reaction. Conner surely meant no

harm, she'd told herself many times over, and there was no need

for her father to frighten him--or worse. Besides, she could

handle him herself.

"You know, Conner, you really shouldn't do such things,"
Maribel tentatively began. "It was a nice gesture, but--"

"But what?" Conner asked, the corners of his smile fading
so that his yellow teeth still remained bared. His dark eyes
became hard as he stared down at her. "Why don't you like the
things I do for you?"

Maribel tried to laugh light-heartedly, but it came out
sounding forced and frightened. "Conner, it's not that--you do
too much for me. I don't deserve such treatment."

"Yes you do," Conner humorlessly insisted. He took another
quick step forward, pressing his tall, thin body into her space.
Suddenly serious, he said, "I would do much more for you, more
than anyone else could, if only you'd allow me."

Repulsed by his near presence, Maribel tried to take a
second step back, but bumped against her father's workbench. She
was cornered. Beginning to feel frightened, she turned her face
away and said, "Conner, please, if you would just--"

"Have supper with me tonight," Conner persisted, leaning his
hand on the workbench beside her so the distance between them was
closed to inches, "I won't take no for an answer, not again--"

Suddenly a glowing sword blade slapped onto the workbench
beside Conner's hand, hissing into the wood. Conner flinched with
surprise and jerked his hand back to his chest like a child
having been caught trying to steal sweets, his eyes wide with
alarm.

"Afternoon, **Conner**," Orion said from across the workbench
with a challenging scowl. The young man turned his

confrontational gaze on his twin sister, then back to Conner.
"Fancy meeting you here. Looking to buy something, are you?"

Conner's look of surprise melted away into a sneer of
contempt as he lowered his hands to his sides. "No, Orion. I'm
not."

"Are you sure, Conner?" Orion persisted, his face glistening
with sweat. He turned the glowing sword up onto its edge and
slowly drew it back, cutting a smoking cleft into the workbench
with a long hiss. "My father and I forge the sharpest blades
around. They can cut a man clean in half...Perhaps I'll give you
a demonstration some time."

Conner took an involuntary step back, his top lip curling
back from his small teeth at Orion's implied threat. "I said I
wasn't interested."

"Fine," Orion said, angrily raising the glowing sword and
pointing it across the street, "Then shove off. And don't let me
see you here again."

Conner nervously licked his lips, his dark eyes shifting to
Maribel. He seemed to want to say something, but then apparently
decided against it and stormed back across the street to finish
stacking rabbit cages.

"O-RION!" Maribel yelled once Conner was gone, wheeling
around to face her brother. "What are you doing? Have you gone
mad?"

"I don't like him around you," Orion said, lowering the
glowing sword back onto the workbench.

"Would you put that thing away?" Maribel said, flinching away from the sword. "Look at yourself--waving around a hot sword like a lunatic! No wonder I've not married yet, with a brother like you scaring all the men off!"

"I'm not scaring anyone off--I'm trying to protect you!"

"Who said I need protection? I certainly didn't ask you for it."

"It doesn't matter. I don't like him."

"Neither do I. But that doesn't give you the right to act like a complete--"

"What's going on here?" Urick interrupted as he came from the rear of the tent to find the two siblings in a heated argument, glaring daggers at one another from across the workbench.

Maribel was the first to break off the searing gaze to look at her father. "Conner and I were talking, and then this...this animal, started waving around a hot sword and threatening to cut people in half."

Troubled, Urick frowned at his son. "Is this true, Orion?" he asked.

Orion scowled at Maribel for a moment longer, then looked to his father and nodded. "It is. I don't like Conner being around her. His intentions are bad."

"See, father? He's crazy!"

"Silence, Maribel," Urick said, holding up his hand. He then tipped his head to Orion and said, "Hurry up and get that blade cooled. If it warps you'll be here all night trying to right it."

Orion pulled the hot sword off the table, scowled once more at his sister--who coldly returned the favor--before striding to his work area and angrily stabbing the blade into the barrel of water with a sharp hiss.

"He's your twin brother, Maribel. You should be grateful you have him. He only means to protect you," Urick said after he was gone.

Maribel rolled her eyes in exasperation and folded her arms. "Father, how will I ever meet a suitor if Orion insists on acting like a madman everytime a man speaks to me?"

Urick smiled as he held out a calloused hand containing the two silver coins. "When you find a man that is worthy of your hand, I promise you, a thousand madmen won't be enough to scare him off."

A reluctant smile gradually appeared on Maribel's face as she reached out and took the coins from him. "Thank you, father. But be sure to give Orion a good talking-to, would you? I'm not a child anymore. He embarrasses me sometimes."

"Sure thing, dear. A harsh punishment it will be," Urick promised, smiling as he watched his daughter hurry off into the village to buy her fabric.

Once she was gone Urick shifted his gaze across the street to where Conner had angrily resumed unloading his rabbits from off his cart, the animals squabbling inside their rattled cages.

Urick's smile faded.

Something about Conner--the way he was always skulking around after the village girls--didn't set right with him. The dark-haired young man was not someone he trusted around his daughter. Not anyone's daughter, for that matter.

"Orion," Urick said as he threw his rag onto the workbench, still staring mistrustfully at Conner while feeling a strong swell of pride for Orion having scared him off, "Let's take a break and go to the pub. My treat."

## CHAPTER 3

"Horris! **HOR-RIS!**" the fat drunk yelled, slamming down his wooden mug and wiping his mouth on the back of his hand. "Bring me another!"

The small, dirt-floored pub in which he sat was just large enough for a bar and a half-dozen rickety wooden tables, most of which were occupied by murmuring noontime patrons. Gray pipe smoke lingered midway in the air like a thin fog, scattered shafts of daylight filtering in through the gaps in the poorly thatched roof.

From the end of the bar Horris came lumbering over wiping out a mug with a soiled rag. "Don't yeh think yeh've already had enough, Guss?" he asked, frowning at the drunk patron. Horris was a giant of a man, with a gleaming shaved head and a short, curly brown beard. He stood well over six feet tall, and was as broad as a field ox.

Guss straightened up from slouching over the bar, his bloodshot eyes drunkenly adrift and his ugly, pock-scarred face twisting with anger. "I'll tell you when...when I've had my fill, damnit!" he spat. "Now fetch me more o' that swill!"

Slowly, Horris set the mug he'd been cleaning aside and said, "You're a mite demandin' for someone drinkin' on credit, don't yeh think?"

Guss slammed his fist on the bar in front of Horris. "I work for a bloody livin'! My own two hands! You know that. My money'sssssgood. An' if I wanna get good an' drunk, damnit, I have the right!"

Horris sighed, noticing that several of his patrons had suspended their conversations to glance towards the ruckus being made at the bar. Calmly, he bent down, folded his meaty forearms on the bartop, and said just loudly enough for Guss to hear, "Guss, yer good and drunk already. Now, I say you pack up and go on home, and don't make no more of it."

His pocked face twisting angrily, Guss spit on the bar in front of him and said, "Who do you think you're--"

Bad idea.

Without warning Horris's massive arms shot out, grabbing two fistfulls of Guss's shirt and dragging him effortlessly over the bar.

"Hey!" Guss shouted as he was handled like a sack of potatoes, "The hell you think you're doing--"

"Aww, shut up, yeh filthy slop," Horris growled as he lugged the struggling drunk across the pub amid encouraging cheers from the patrons. Kicking open the rickety door, Horris dragged Guss outside by the scruff of his neck and hurled him into the busy street, villagers and squabbling chickens scattering out of the way.

"An' don't come back till yer paid up, neither!" Horris said, slapping his hands clean.

Just then Urick and Orion appeared, walking together down the street. Horris saw them and his face instantly lit up, revealing a missing front tooth which had been knocked out years ago during a brawl with five men.

"Afternoon, you two! Whaddaya doin' here?" Horris asked, suddenly quite pleasant.

Urick held up the basket as he neared. "Took a break for lunch. Thought we'd come visit."

On the ground Guss groaned as he awkwardly got to his feet, coughed out a mouthful of dust, and staggered off.

"Busy day, I see?" Urick asked humorously as he watched Guss amble unsteadily away down the street. The angry drunk tried kicking at a dog in his path, missed, and nearly crashed once more into the dirt.

Horris batted a dismissive hand. "Nah. That's just Guss-- Does this every now an' then. Mean drunk, see. He'll be fine in the mornin'." Horris then turned to Orion and said, "Fancy seein' you here, lad! Yer father ain't workin' yeh too hard, is he?"

"As always, uncle," Orion conceaded.

"Good. Maybe one day he'll turn you into a man after all!"
he said, slapping the young man on the shoulder with the force to
stagger him to the side. Laughing heartily, Horris then rubbed
his ample gut, took in a breath, and asked the two, "Well then,
who fancies a mug o' me fine ale?"

Back inside the pub Urick and Orion were seated at the bar
eating their lunch when Horris slid two sloshing mugs of heady
ale across to them. "There. Try somma that. It's my freshest
brew--jus' been tapped," the big man said with a wink.

Orion picked up his mug and took a healthy swallow. The
young man forced it down with a shiver and coughed into his fist.
"Not bad, uncle," he said, his voice slightly constrained.

"Not the worst you've brewed, that's for sure," Urick
admitted, tipping his mug to Horris before taking a sip of the
heady, amber liquid to wash down the salt pork.

Horris's eyebrows bent into a frown as he scratched
something in his curly brown beard. "An' just what's that 'posed
to mean?" he demanded.

Horris's brew was widely known to be the most foul-tasting,
rot-gut swill in the entire village. His ale was sour enough to
pucker a drunkard's lips, and his mead was so dark and thick it
was like drinking syrup. But no one could brew alcohol stronger,
nor sell it any cheaper, which was what kept the pub in business
and prevented the local drunks from ever walking straight. Horris
took great pride in this, and never reacted well to criticism of
his alcohol.

Just then a slovenly-looking man sitting across the room

leaned off his stool and vomitted on the dirt floor. On cue every
patron inside the pub lifted their mugs and cheered: In
Horris's pub, the first spew of the day always called for a
celebration.

Horris lowered his mug, chuckling as he watched the drunken
man amble off towards the door clutching his stomach. When Horris
turned back he noticed Urick and Orion humorously shaking their
heads with mutual laughter. "What?" Horris asked incredulously,
realizing they were laughing at his expense. "A good spew means
it's quality ale...It does!...Ah, piss off, the both of yeh. I
like it," he relented, flipping a hand and raising his mug to his
mouth.

Although not related by blood, and about as opposite in
nature as any two men could possibly be, Urick and Horris were as
close as brothers. Having grown up together from boyhood, the two
had always enjoyed one another's company. Horris's lighthearted
friendship had given Urick a reprieve from his father's stern
labor in the smithy, while Urick's reliable nature had given
Horris an escape from his father's drunken beatings. Despite
following the basic paths of their fathers, the two had continued
to remain close friends over the years, each living somewhat
vicariously through the other for the gaps missing in their
lives: Urick coming to the pub to relax from long day of labor;
Horris becoming a godfather in place of the family he'd never
had.

Chuckling, Urick set his mug down, wiping ale foam from his
mouth with a grimy hand as he turned to his son. "Orion, why

don't you show your uncle the dagger you've been working on?" he
suggested.

Looking just slightly embarrassed, Orion reached back,
slipped his hand under the tail of his shirt, and produced a
long, double-edged dagger which he laid on the bar.

"Orion, lad, yeh made this?" Horris asked with amazement. He
set down his mug and picked up the dagger to examine it, the
slight to his ale completely forgotten.

"Just finished it. Turned out a lot better than my last
one," Orion admitted. "Took me four days."

The dagger blade was perfectly symmetrical, the flawless
steel winking in the dim, smoke-filled light of the pub. The
handle was beautifully crafted of three thick bands of interwoven
copper ending at a polished silver cap. The craftsmanship was
that expected of a seasoned blacksmith, not a young man earning
his apprenticeship beneath his father.

"I taught him too much," Urick said, giving a proud half-
smile. "One of these days he's going to put me out of business,
I'm sure of it."

"I knowd it!" a man suddenly yelled from across the pub,
slapping a pair of dice off a table and standing up, pointing
accusingly at his burly gambling partner. "I knowd you was a
lousy cheat!"

"The hell'd you jus' call me?" the other man asked,
shooting up to his feet with his chin jutted angrily forward.

"You heard me! I saw you palmin' the dice--Twice now yeh
done it!"

"You best watch yer tongue, 'fore I rip the bloody thing
outta yer head!"

"Well come an' get it then, yeh **FILTHY CHEAT!**"

Hearing the argument between the two patrons, and knowing
what would soon follow, Urick and Orion each casually covered
their mugs with their hands as they continued eating lunch.

Not a second later Horris stood and slammed his fist on the
bar with the force to make bowls hop and mugs slosh clear down
the length of the counter. The entire pub startled into abrupt
silence, Horris then leaned over the bar, pointing the gleaming
dagger back and forth between the two quarreling gamblers.
"You two best take it outside or let it die, 'cause if yeh don't,
so help me, I'll wallop the daft right outta yeh both. You know
the rules. This here's a peaceful establishment, damnit!"

Seeing the monstrous man holding the sharp dagger, the two
gamblers hesitated, then wisely sank back down into their chairs.
Half-heartedly they exchanged grumbled apologies as they
obediently resumed their game of dice.

Horris continued to scowl menacingly at the two men for a
moment longer. Then, as abruptly as when he'd thrown Guss out on
the street, Horris smiled pleasantly as he turned back to his
brother and nephew. "Ha! Wouldja look at that? Waggin' this thing
at 'em shuts 'em right up." He flipped the dagger over and caught
it by the blade, offering it back to Orion handle-first with an
approving nod of his bald, scar-pitted head. "Right good job,
lad. 'N fact, what say one of these days you make me one? I'd pay
good money for a knife like that."

"Sure thing," Orion said, taking the dagger and tucking it back into his waistband. He popped a piece of salt pork in his mouth and smiled at his father as he chewed. "You see that? My first real customer."

"What did I tell you?" Urick said to Horris, "The boy's already putting me out of business."

For the next half hour the three sat at the bar talking as they ate lunch, their conversations occasionally interrupted by Horris refilling mugs or barking at drunks to mind their manners. One man passed out at his table and began to snore loudly, so Horris picked him up in his arms like a sleeping child and dumped him outside. It was almost humorous watching the big man manage the pub, like watching a hideous nanny looking after her brood of delinquent children.

Horris had just finished collecting a tab when he leaned over the bar to speak quietly to Orion. "I noticed there's a prettly little lass over there. Been watching you," he said, nodding discreetly across the way.

Interested, Orion set down his mug and slyly craned his neck over his shoulder to see the girl his uncle had mentioned.

Across the smoky pub a buxom woman sat at a table looking in their direction. Her dress was stained, her greasy hair matted on one side as if she'd just woken up, and one of her eyes was blackenëd. Seeing that she'd caught the attention of the two men at the bar, she smiled with crooked teeth and twiddled her fingersśin a flirtatious wave.

Orion's head whipped around in disgust. "I'd rather not!" he said, shaking his head as he busied himself with the last bit of his salt pork.

"You sure?" Urick teased his son. "Another round of your uncle's brew, and I'd bet she'd look like a goddess."

"Yer damned right she would," Horris agreed, winking at the slovenly woman from over his mug as he sipped his ale. Then he turned his attention to Urick and asked, "What about you, eh? When you gonna find yerself a woman?"

The amused look on Urick's dirty face melted away. For a long moment he fixed Horris with a pointed stare from across the bar, then set down his mug and pushed back his chair. "It's time we get back to work," he announced.

'Nice job,' Orion mouthed to Horris from across the bar.

"Aww!" Horris complained, realizing he'd struck a nerve in his brother without even meaning to do so. "Common, yeh know I didn't mean nothin' by it! I've been drinkin' all day--bit woozy is all. Stay a while and have another, on me. What say we make a day of it?"

"Not today," Urick said as he stood up, openly irritated with his friend. The comment about finding a woman had obviously rubbed him the wrong way--as it always did. He glanced at his son. "We really should get back. Need to finish those bridles."

Knowing it was useless once Urick was angry, Horris shrugged his shoulders and collected the empty mugs without further objection. "Fine, have it yer way. But do me a favor, wouldja?

Tell Maribel I send my love. I haven't seen that girl in a fortnight..." Horris's bushy eyebrows frowned as he trailed off, troubled by his niece's absence. "She never stops by much anymore, now that I think of it."

A hint of humor showing through his irritation, Urick said, "That's because I told her not to come within eyesight of this place."

Horris appeared slightly affronted at this, but then nodded with understanding as he studied the seamy quality of patrons which filled his pub on a daily basis. "Yeah...Prob'ly a good idea, that," he admitted. A young woman as sweet and beautiful as Maribel had no business coming here.

Orion and Urick said their goodbyes, and as they were leaving through the pub's rickety door they heard Horris yell from behind them, "Damnit, Ben! If you pull that thing out one more time, I swear I'm gonna rip it off an' slap yeh with it!"

CHAPTER 4

Their stomachs full and their thirst quenched, Urick and
Orion strolled through the village at an unhurried walk back to
the smithy.

The village had been established in a tall meadow of grass,
backed by a ridge of lush green mountains on one side and a
massive, scenically sparkling lake on the other. At this time of
day fishermen were coming and going in their canoes from the
rocky bank, hauling in nets and hanging trout on racks to dry in
the warm afternoon sun. A line of women with their gowns hitched
up squatted at the water's edge, gossipping and laughing amongst
themselves as they scrubbed clothes. Children ran giggling throug
through the tall grass on the village edge, chasing one another
about. Not far away a hunter emerged from the dense treeline at
the foot of the mountains with a deer slumped across his shoulder

shoulders and a longbow in his hands.

Together Urick and Orion strolled past the rows of mud and
thatch huts into the small village market. Alongside the dirt
lane that ran through the village, a small number of vendors and
merchants gathered daily to peddle their wares and haggle over
prices. Tables were erected on which clay jugs of milk, wheels of
cheese, fresh cuts of mutton, baskets of eggs, sacks of grain,
and mounds of fruit were put on display. Goats bleated, chickens
squabbled, dogs barked, and pigs snuffled in the dust. Men led
mules down the busy street pulling cartloads of hay, sloshing
buckets of water, and long planks of wood. Above it all the warm
afternoon air was fragrant with the smells of freshly baked bread
and flame-cooked meat.

"I was wondering," Orion said as he strolled through the
market beside his father, "Would it be alright if I left work
early tomorrow?"

"What for?" Urick asked. It wasn't often--if ever--that the
boy neglected his responsibilities.

Orion grinned as he stared ahead, already knowing his father
was about to give him trouble. "There's...there's a girl,
Samantha, I just met. I was hoping to spend the afternoon with
her, if I could get the time off."

"Ahh...when you'd meet her?" Urick inquired. He enjoyed
speaking to his son about girls. Orion was practically a full-
grown man now, and the realm of women and relationships was one
of the precious few areas he could still offer his son guidance.
This was much more enjoyable than speaking with Maribel about men

and childbirth--something he absolutely detested and avoided at all costs.

"I met her last week, when I was delivering Frank's horseshoes. She's his daughter," Orion explained.

Urick smiled, remembering himself thinking it had taken his son an awfully long time to make that delivery. "A nice girl, I presume?"

Orion suppressed a grin, his green eyes twinkling with humor as they walked past the butcher's shop of hanging beef slabs. "Yes father, she's a very nice girl."

"And what are your plans for tomorrow, hmm?" Urick persisted, good-naturedly needling his son.

Orion shrugged. "I was thinking of borrowing Jeremy's canoe and taking her out on the water. What do you think?"

"Not bad," Urick said, impressed. "She'll like that. I took your mother out hunting squirrels on our first date."

Orion laughed at the joke, but then glanced over and saw that his father was serious. "And that worked?" he asked, amazed, "Hunting squirrels?"

Urick leaned in to Orion as they walked and said quietly, "You're here, aren't you?"

"Ugh!" Orion cringed in humorous disgust.

Urick laughed and clapped Orion on the back, about to give his blessing for the date, when the sunlight suddenly dimmed. It was as if the sun had abruptly lost its power, casting the world below into gloom. In an instant, all the bustling activity in the small village ceased, silence cutting like a knife through the midday ruckus. Fearfully, the shadowy face of every villager was instinctively turned skyward.

There, soaring through the sky like an angry leviathan come to spread its wrath, was a monstrous dragon. It's mighty wings spread so wide they eclipsed the sun, its long barbed tail flowing in the air behind it, the terrible beast arched its long neck and let out a roar so powerful that it shook the sky like thunder.

As if frozen by terror the villagers stood in rigid silence, faces upturned and eyes widening, unable to break the terrible paralysis that cemented their feet to the ground as the dragon swept down from the sky, its nightmarish body growing larger by the second.

Finally, a woman dropped a basket of eggs at her feet and screamed, "It's Temper! Everybody--**RUN!**"

Then all hell broke loose.

CHAPTER 5

Temper swept down from the sky, smashing a cart in an
explosion of boards under his mammoth weight as he landed on the
lake's edge. The dragon's plated scales flared menacingly as he
then arched his serpentine neck, massive jaws stretching wide as
he roared a column of blue-orange flame down onto the village,
engulfing a row of huts in flame.

Chaos erupted.

Women screamed and ran to find their crying children,
scooping them up into their arms as they fled. Men yelled in
alarm, abandoning their work and running to find their families,
free their livestock, or arm themselves with weapons. Several
dove into the lake and began splashing away, hoping to find
refuge in the water.

Temper's fearsomely horned head reared back, slit-pupiled

eyes gleaming as viciously as rubys as he watched the villagers
scattering in terror before him.

Below a man ducked out of the doorway of his hut to see what
the commotion was, his face paling with horror and his eyes
widening up at the snarling dragon. Before he could run Temper
struck at him with snake-like speed, plucking him off the ground
and swallowing him whole.

"Leave us, you monster!" a man yelled over the panicked
screams, pulling back his bow and taking aim at Temper's chest.
When he released the bowstring the arrow hissed through the air
and clicked harmlessly off of Temper's armored scales, leaving
not even a scratch.

Temper's head whipped around, slitted eyes blazing
demoniacally, sword-length teeth bared in a fiery snarl at the
foolish man who'd dared challenge him.

Seeing that his arrow had been useless against the dragon's
might, the man threw down his bow and tried to run just as Temper
reared back and blew a roiling column of flame down at him. A
split second later the man was a horribly screaming fireball
which flailed and stumbled in the street, panicked villagers
fleeing all around him.

A disoriented child separated from his family in the
confusion stood screaming in the street. In their wild
desperation to flee, villagers pushed over carts and tables
standing in their way, spilling stacks of bread, dried racks of
fish, bushels of plumbs and apples as they stampeded through the
marketplace. One old man was shoved aside and fell onto his

stomach as boots and bare feet pounded the life from his frail
body. One man was running for cover when Temper's thick tail
close-lined him across the middle and smashed him through a mud
wall.

"Help me! Someone!" a pregnant woman cried as she hurried
clumsily down the street, holding her bulging stomach with one
hand while grasping for help with the other. All around her
people were running past, much too frightened of the dragon
tearing its way through the village to notice her.

Not far away a row of huts exploded in a wall of fire as
Temper raked the village with volcanic eruptions of flame. The
stench of cooked flesh and burning huts rose with the hellish
screams of the frightened and dying, acrid black smoke filling
the air.

The pregnant woman desperately grabbed a man's pantleg as
he swung up onto his whinnying, wild-eyed horse. "Please help
me!" she begged, frightened tears streaking her face, "I can't-"

"Find your own way out, woman!" the man snarled, kicking her
down as he spurred his horse away through the village.

Sobbing, the pregnant woman had just managed to climb to her
feet when Temper's horned head rose above the flames behind her
like a nightmarish serpent. The woman turned, cradling her
bulging stomach with both arms as if to protect the unborn child
inside.

"Please, don't hurt me, mighty Temper!" she pleaded as she
backed away from the dragon, "I'm with child; Surely you

wouldn't--"

Temper turned his head sideways and struck through the
flames, his jaws slamming shut around her middle with the muffled
snap of bones and the wet pop of flesh as he mercilessly threw
back his head and swallowed her whole.

"Oh God...oh God...oh God...," a man with sweat dripping off
his face uttered as he stood on a flat cart, frantically pulling
off caged chickens to save what he could of his stock as
screaming villagers stampeded past. Just then Temper came
smashing through a row of burning huts, hot embers swirling in
the air as the dragon wreaked havoc upon the village.

"OhGodohGodohGodohGodOHGODOHGOD**OHGODOHGOD**!" the man panicked
as the dragon neared, turning to jump down off the cart with a
bundle of squabbling chickens held in his arms.

Too late.

Temper's armor-plated tail--as long and thick as a tree--
smashed down on the opposite end of the cart, launching the man
and his chickens high into the air with the force of a catapult.

Crawling forward through the village on low, powerful
haunches, Temper snarled as yellow flames licked through his
razor-sharp teeth, his slitted red eyes searching the devastation
before him for more victims.

CHAPTER 6

Screaming and yelling in terror, waves of peasants fled the village and went tearing across the meadow, running for the safety of the densly forested hills. Looming nightmarishly behind them, Temper continued to destroy everything in his path, wr wreaking havoc on the burning village as he smashed through huts, roared intense columns of flame, feasting on any livestock or humans unfortunate enough to have been caught in his path.

Urick and Orion were amongst those in the scattered crowds running across the meadow towards the safety of the forest when suddenly Urick stopped short. Sweating, panting, Urick turned in quick half-circle, his worried eyes frantically scanning the panicked faces of the villagers running through the tall grass all around him.

Realizing his father wasn't with him, Orion turned back

also, frantic and bewildered. "Father! What are you doing? Let's
go!" he yelled from up ahead, his sweaty face glistening gold.

Amongst the burning huts Temper reared back his horned head
and swallowed an entire horse as he continued on his rampage.

Urick, the worry on his face now bordering on panick,
continued to search the hysterical faces of those fleeing past
with frantic darts of his eyes. "Maribel!" he yelled to his son,
"I don't see Maribel!"

A look of horror tensed Orion's face as he realized he
hadn't seen Maribel either. For several moments both of them
stood in the meadow, turning in circles as they called out
Maribel's name, searching for her in the horrified groups of
villagers running all around them.

Then Urick turned to his son and barked, "Orion, get into
the forest and see if you can find her there. I'm going back to
look for her!"

"She's safe if she's in the forest. If she's still in the
village it'll take both of us to find her--I'm going with you!"
Orion shouted as Temper released yet another ground-trembling
roar.

Urick didn't have time to argue. All that mattered was
finding Maribel and getting her to safety. He could not--**would
not**--allow Temper to harm her.

"Fine!" Urick shouted, "Follow me!"

Side by side they began running through the meadow against
the flow of panicked villagers fleeing in the opposite direction.
One of them was a screaming woman, a trail of smoke flowing off

her charred hair. Another was a staggering, pale-faced man
clutching a bloody stump where his arm should have been.

"Maribel!" Urick called out through cupped hands as he came
jogging into the ruin which had been the village market.
"Maribel, can you hear me? MARIBEL!"

The black smoke made it impossible to see far. The sounds
were horrendous. Temper, concealed within the smoke and flame of
his own destruction, roared like a thing from hell as he
continued on his rampage through the village. Pigs released
ear-splitting squeels as they fought to escape their pins.
Wild-eyed horses whinnied and bucked their heads against their
tethers. Fire roared and crackled. The wounded left helplessly in
the cluttered, smoke-filled streets screamed in pain.

Barely able to hear himself speak, Urick grabbed Orion's
shoulder and yelled over the terrible sounds filling the searing
hot air, "We have to find her! Stay close to me!"

Together they searched through the village, jogging amid
acrid black drifts of smoke and around overturned barrels,
demolished huts, and destroyed shops, checking everywhere for
Maribel.

"Maribel, can you hear me? Where are you?" Urick called out,
raising his grime-blackened hand to shield his face from the heat
of a roaring fire beside him.

All that Urick saw moving through the heat-shimmering air
ahead was a donkey, braying with terror as it loped past pulling
a flaming cart behind it. Across the street Orion shoved over a

flaming plank of wood, coughing and waving smoke from his face as
he found a man underneath. Charred. Dead.

"She's not here," Urick said, swallowing his terror and
trying to slow his racing mind enough to think. Maribel had been
on her way to...to what? To what? To buy cloth! But from who?
**From who?**"

"Isabel!" Urick shouted, suddenly remembering the name
Maribel had given him earlier in the day. He turned to his son
and asked with a tremor in his voice, "Orion, do you know where
Isabel lives?"

Orion frowned, his eyes darting with frantic thought in his
sweat-sheened face. "I...at--at the other end of the market, I
think," he said, "She and her husband--"

"Come on!" Urick barked, tearing off with startling speed.

One after the other they sprinted through the destroyed
market, leaping through licking flames and clambering over
rubble. A wagon which had been crashed into a shop by a panicked
driver blocked the lane ahead. The two were about to jog around
it when suddenly Urick said, "Get down...!" and pulled Orion down
behind the wagon.

Not far away Temper rose his massive head above the flames,
blood and scraps of flesh streaking his scaled muzzle. His fiery
reptilian eyes searched the devastation below, his nostrils
flaring as he scented the air, searching for another victim among
the ruin.

Laying on their stomachs beneath the wagon, Urick and Orion

could only hold their breath and wait, hoping the dragon would
move on without noticing them.

After a moment Temper jerked his awful head to the side and
snarled, revealing gore-streaked teeth as he took notice of
something elsewhere in the village. Lowering his head like a
predator on the hunt, the dragon then stalked off between the
burning huts, his huge scaled body vanishing in a swirl of black
smoke.

"He's gone. Let's go!" Urick said to Orion, scrambling out
from beneath the wagon and continuing to run through the market.

The two hadn't gone much further when Orion grabbed his
father's shirt and pointed to an open-faced shop half collapsed
amid the destruction. "That's Isabel's shop--I'm sure of it!"
Orion shouted as the thatch roof of a burning hut across the lane
fell in on itself, throwing bright red embers high into the air.

"Start looking--she's got to be around here somewhere!"
Urick said, frantically beginning to search the rubble in the
area as he repeatedly yelled out Maribel's name. Concern for his
own life vanished--Urick had to find his daughter, even if he
died trying to do so.

"Maribel!" Orion shouted, covering his nose and mouth with
the crook of his arm as smoke stung his eyes. He took in a
lungful of the acrid, searing hot air and began to cough--which
was why he almost didn't hear the faint moan coming from a pile
of rubble nearby.

Coughing harshly, Orion hurried over to the rubble and

shoved aside a handcart. Underneath, laying on her back and half-
buried in crumbled mud bricks, was Maribel, looking dirty and
dazed with a bleeding gash on her temple.

"Father! She's over here!" Orion shouted as he began digging
the rubble off his sister with both hands.

Urick ran over and dropped to his knees, his rough,
calloused hands trembling as he touched Maribel's beautiful face.
"Maribel, my angel, you're safe. We're going to get you out,"
he promised.

Maribel responded by moaning, her bloodied lips sluggishly
attempting to form unintelligible words.

Once enough rubble had been cleared off of her, Urick picked
up Maribel's limp body as if she weighed nothing and draped her
over his shoulder. "We got her--Let's get out of here!" he
shouted, turning back the way they'd come, Maribel's body
bouncing limply across his shoulder as he ran.

They made it to the butcher's shop--now a roaring mass of
flame--and could just see the meadow's edge through the thick
smoke on the far end of the village.

"Almost there, Maribel. Almost," Urick panted as he ran with
his unconscious daughter towards safety.

He nearly made it.

Just as Urick was nearing the edge of the village a
monstrous shadow, imposed over the rubble-strewn ground by the
wavering glow of the many fires burning all around, suddenly rose
up behind him.

Urick's legs stiffened as the searing heat disappeared from the surface of his skin and was replaced by a cold chill which turned his sweat to frost. The hairs on the back of his neck stood on end and goosebumps prickled the length of his arms as the looming shadow, as well as the sinister presence accompanying it, grew closer behind him. Urick stood stone solid amid the burning ruin as he held Maribel's body draped over his shoulder, closing his eyes and praying to the Gods that Temper hadn't seen them.

But on this day, the Gods weren't listening.

Only yards away Temper reared back his long neck like a coiled serpent ready to strike, his blazing red eyes narrowing to slits. The dragon's jaws flashed viciously open, his black forked tongue slithering hungrily across his razor-sharp teeth as he prepared to devour the two foolish mortals who thought they could escape his wrath.

Temper's head had just begun its downward strike when a voice yelled out, "NO!" and a small, flashing object hissed through the air.

Temper roared with furious pain and jerked back his head, a copper-handled dagger buried in the soft tissue around his nostril--one of the few places on his body not plated with thick scales.

A momentary look of horror crossed Orion's features as he stood in the rubble-strewn street ahead, realizing the dire consequences of what he'd just done. But just as quickly the young man summoned his courage in order to save his father and sister and yelled, "Over here, you cursed demon! Come and get

me!"

"Orion!" Urick yelled in horror, wanting to run to his boy

but unable to leave his helpless daughter. "Orion--**RUN!**"

Urick's voice was drowned out when Temper turned his lethal

gaze onto Orion and released a furious roar that shook the

ground. Then Temper unfolded his giant wings, and with one

powerful beat took to the air in a swirl of flames and embers.

Stumbling, Orion turned and began racing through the ruined

village as fast as he could, hurtling smouldering piles of

rubble and ducking beneath shattered roofs. Not far behind Temper

swept down, stretching open his fearsome mouth and roaring a ball

of flame at the young fool who'd dared oppose him.

Feeling the heat of the flame, Orion dove behind a trough of

water and covered his head with both arms.

Just then the fireball struck the ground with the force of a

comet, engulfing everything in the area with searing hot flames.

Amongst the roaring fire Orion pushed himself up and looked out

over the now boiling trough of water, his green eyes darting with

fear as he watched Temper bank in the smoke-filled sky for

another pass.

His heart hammering with panic, Orion sprang to his feet and

ran through the scorching flames with his head down, hardly

feeling their heat licking his skin. The sleeve of his shirt

caught fire, and as he ran through the rubble-strewn street he

cursed and beat out the flames.

Not far behind Temper cut a swirling path through the smoky

air, his razor-sharp talons flashing open as he descended on the
boy.

Orion never saw it coming.

Luckily, something caught Orion's foot and sent him crashing
hard to the dirt. Not a heartbeat later Temper swept by so low
that Orion's clothes rippled in the turbulence, the dragon's
hooked talons just missing him and ripping two gaping chunks from
a stone wall ahead.

Orion got to his feet wincing, pausing for a brief moment
when he realized that what he'd fallen over was the scorched body
of a woman, her blistered lips cooked away from her teeth in a
melted scream, her sunken eyesockets still smouldering. Then in
the next instant Orion's attention was wrenched from the grisly
scene of death as Temper landed ahead, serpentine neck whipping
around and his slitted red eyes narrowing murderously down at
him.

The dead woman and the pain of his sprained ankle forgotten,
Orion cursed and tore off down the street as the hulking dragon
came smashing forward through the devastation after him. Orion ra
ran as fast as his legs would carry him, but still the dragon
closed on him with long, powerful strides which trembled the
ground. Orion hurtled a barrel and fell onto his rear, sliding
beneath a cartload of melons. At the same instant Temper dropped
his head and raked his horns, lifting the cart and throwing it
high through the air.

Stumbling to his feet, Orion cut down an alley just as
Temper blew a river of blue-orange flame down at him, reducing a

hut into a wall of fire with an awesome explosion of heat.
Momentarily out of the dragon's line of sight due to the flames,
Orion raced down the narrow alley and slid in behind a rickety
shed to his left, using his forearm to wipe sweat from his eyes
as he gasped for breath, his heart racing in the tight confines
of his chest.

Temper was not far behind. The dragon's horned, diamond-
shaped head snaked through the flames, turning his red eyes into
fiery slits. He bared his gore-streaked teeth, his nostrils
flexing as he scented the air for the human who'd dared smite
him, whose flesh he craved.

His back pressed up against the rickety shed, Orion
attempted to slow his breathing while simultaneously struggling
not to cough against the thick smoke drifting in the hot air. He
could feel the dragon's hungry presence from only yards away.
Orion squeezed his eyes shut and tilted his head back to breathe
silently, sweat draining off his face and running in rivulets
down his throat.

Temper's fiery eyes shifted from side to side, searching the
narrow alleyway for the human. The air was filled with the
overlapping smells of death, fear, and ruin. Finding it difficult
to locate the human's scent in the midst of his own destruction,
Temper snarled and retracted his head through the flames to
search for the elusive human elsewhere.

Sensing that Temper had gone, Orion risked a quick glance
around the side of the shed. Through the shimmering yellow flames
he saw the scaled end of the dragon's tail sliding away as Temper

continued on down the street. With a knot of worry still pulsing
in his throat, Orion pushed away from the shed and ran crouched
at the waist down the narrow alley, keeping low. He veered in
between two huts and jumped over a gate into an empty pig's pen,
trying to get as far away from the dragon's path of destruction
as possible. Running across the muddy plot he again leapt the
gate and jogged to a horse stable.

     There Orion's body finally gave way under the fatigue of
having been chased through the village by Temper, the waning
adrenaline making his legs tremble and his knees weak. His lungs
ached from the smoke. His head spun. His heart felt like a
hummingbird beating inside his rib cage.

     But despite this Orion coughed out a laugh of disbelief as
he stood bent over with his hands on his trembling knees, still
struggling for breath as sweat rolled off his face. He'd smited
Temper--And lived to tell about it! Orion doubted anyone had ever
done such a thing. It had been deathly foolish, he realized now,
but at the moment he'd seen no other way of rescuing his family
and had acted on pure impulse. His father was going to **kill** him,
Orion knew. Then he thought about what the girls in the village
were going to think when they heard about this. He'd be a hero!
If **this** didn't impress Samantha, nothing would--

     The stable Orion was hiding behind suddenly imploded as
Temper swooped down through a black cloud of smoke and landed
with an earth-trembling impact, demolishing the wood structure
beneath his weight.

Orion was thrown forward by the impact and went sprawling across the ground. The young man had just enough time to roll onto his back, his green eyes wide with fear, and try scrambling away.

Before he got anywhere Temper released a fiery snarl of rage and struck at him with viper-like speed. Orion only had time to hold up his arms and yell before he was ripped from the ground with the wet crunch of bones and swallowed whole.

Then Temper roared one last column of flame over the destroyed village for good measure, unfolded his gigantic wings, and took to the air, disappearing into the black swirls of the smoke-filled sky.

CHAPTER 7

Slowly, cautiously, and in breathless silence, the villagers
began to emerge from the dense treeline at the meadow's edge.

Before them their village lay in ruins. Dozens of fires
burned. Huts were reduced to heaps of strewn rubble. Panicked
livestock ran free in confusion. Distant cries of the injured
rose with the thick black smoke snaking in tendrils into the
crisp blue sky.

The villagers stared in disbelief. Some covered their faces
in horror. Others sank to their knees and began to sob, their
meager lives destroyed. It was as if an angry God had come and
destroyed their world for no reason at all, leaving them with
nothing but sorrow.

One of the first to venture from the cover of the forest was
Horris, carrying a keg of his freshest ale under each of his

massive arms. In the confusion of the attack, they were the only things he'd thought to save. He stopped to survey the devastation with a disgusted grimace and thought, Damn that dragon...Damn that dragon straight to hell where he came from.

Shaking his head in sad regret for all of those who'd surely been killed in this most recent attack, Horris hefted the ale kegs in his arms and began trudging through the tall grass to see what could be salvaged amid the ruin. He was halfway across the meadow when he saw a familiar silhouette moving within the scattered fires and passing clouds of smoke drifting through the village ahead.

"Urick!" Horris bellowed when he recognized his brother emerging from the ruin carrying Maribel's limp body over his shoulder. Terrified, Horris dropped the ale kegs at his feet and raced forward towards them. "Urick! My God--I thought you'd made it out with the others. Is Maribel alright?"

"She'll be fine...Just bumped her head," Urick said quietly. His face was sheened with sweat and soot, and there were burns scorched across his arms and face. His eyes were glazed and distant as he continued walking past his brother and away from the destroyed village.

Horris didn't understand. Temper had just ravaged their village in one of his worst attacks, and Maribel had survived with nothing more than a bumped head. Urick should be thankfull, not acting as though...

A lead weight landing in the pit of his stomach, Horris turned and looked at Urick with fearful eyes. "Urick...where's

Orion?" he asked, his words laced with mounting fear.

Urick stopped in the grass, Maribel's limp upper body slumped unconsciously over his shoulder, her bare arms and long brown hair draped down his broad back. Without turning, Urick said in a low voice just loud enough to be heard over the hissing, popping flames, "He...he saved us."

And with that, Urick continued on into the meadow through scattered groups of villagers cautiously making their way back towards the village.

"No...," Horris muttered, looking from his brother to the burning village and then back again. "NO!"

With a speed that defied his sheer size, Horris tore off into the village in a panicked search for his only nephew. "Orion!" he bellowed, holding up his massive forearm and squinting against the heat of the flames. "Orion! Where are yeh, boy? Say somethin'!"

Nearby a hog was screaming as it laid kicking on the ground, its hide charred black.

Coughing against the foul smoke, Horris hurried through the village, desperately looking everywhere for his nephew.

"Help me," a man with a bloodied face groaned as he limped forward holding his side.

Horris brushed past the wounded man without a second thought. At least he was still alive and walking. His nephew might not be so fortunate.

Seeing a pair of legs protruding out from under an

overturned wagon, Horris ran over and stopped beside it, praying
that if it was Orion underneath that he was alright.

"Don' worry boy! I'll getcha out," he said. He crouched
down, grabbed the bottom side of the wagon, and with an awesome
surge of strength and a bellowing roar flipped the wagon over
onto its side.

Underneath was an ashen-faced man laying in a pool of his
own blood, most of his torso missing from a monstrous bite wound.
It wasn't Orion.

Stepping over the dead man, Horris continued on into the
burning ruins of the village, calling out Orion's name and
hastily searching piles of rubble in the hopes that his nephew
had survived. Numerous fires raged with unbearable heat. The
black smoke stung his eyes and burned his lungs, but still he
continued on.

It wasn't until Horris saw a small object glimmering in the
rubble-strewn street ahead that the hope for his nephew's safety
drained from his heart like sour ale from a tapped keg.

It was Orion's dagger. The same one he'd spent so much time
crafting, the same one Urick had been so proud to show off as an
example of his son's incredible skills. The finely-made knife was
laying in the dirt, its ornate copper handle gleaming in the
firelight, its double-edged blade covered in glistening dragon's
blood.

Mindless of the devastation surrounding him, Horris lumbered
forward as if in a dream and fell to his knees beside the dagger.

"Orion...," he said, tears welling in his eyes and his wide chest hitching as he scooped up the knife in both hands, cradling it like a precious object. "Oh God, Orion, no..."

Then Horris lowered his bearded chin to his chest, squeezed his eyes shut against the awful pain, and began to cry as the village continued to burn all around him.

CHAPTER 8

Temper came gliding down out of the sky, beating his vast
wings and landing with graceful ease on the castle's balcony.

The castle, a white stone fortress perched atop a craggy
ridge, overlooked the rolling green lowlands for miles around. At
one time an exquisitely noble adornment to the lush Scottish
countryside, a beacon promising justice and prosperity while
under the care of king Warrington, the once majestic castle now
resembled a domicile of the dead. Filth-blackened flags whipped
tatterdly in the gusting breeze atop the towering, sharp stone
spires. Jagged shards of stained glass hung in empty black
windows, lifeless and staring. Thick ropes of green ivy snaked
their way up the outer walls.

With pale flesh visible between the green scales of his
bloated underbelly, Temper lumbered his way across the balcony

and through the massive double doors into the king's chambers,
his thick tail dragging behind him.

The king's chambers was a sprawling expanse of marble
illuminated by a towering wall of stained-glass windows which
overlooked the rolling hills below. In the dazzling, multi-
colored beams of light, Temper's heaping mound of gold, jewels,
and countless other treasures stolen from the king gleamed like
the riches of the Gods.

Made lethargic by his bellyfull of villagers and livestock,
Temper crawled atop his glimmering nest of treasures, nestled
down, and curled his thick tail around himself. Before he laid
down his head to sleep, Temper opened his fearsome mouth in a
yawn and flicked a morsel of flesh out of his teeth with his
black forked tongue.

Not far away a shred of Orion's dark-haired scalp splattered
onto the marble floor.

CHAPTER 9

Kneeling down, Urick gently lowered Orion's dagger into a shallow hole in the ground. Then he pushed a mound of dark soil in over the top of it and carefully began stacking a small pile of stones over the disturbed patch of ground. Once finished, he stood up and wiped his hands clean without a single word, his face grimly stoic as he stared down at the makeshift grave.

"God be with yeh, boy," Horris said. His bald head was bowed, tears streaming down his cheeks and into the brown curls of his beard as he fought back sobs which hitched in his broad chest. At his side Maribel stood weeping unconsolably, her face cupped in her hands.

The three of them stood at the far end of the meadow furthest from the village, just at the edge of the forest of evergreens. Scattered throughout the meadow a dozen other

families stood huddled in mournful groups around the fresh graves
of their loved ones. The morning dew was just beginning to
evaporate with the early morning sun, ghostly tendrils of mist
rising from the meadow like spirits departing amid the sounds of
sorrowful weeping.

"I was awful to him," Maribel managed to say, wiping tears
from the corners of her puffy, reddened eyes. A bruise darkened
her temple, the result of being knocked unconscious beneath the
pile of rubble. "He protected me, always, but I...I..." Maribel
couldn't finish. She returned her face to her hands, weeping
uncontrollably.

Urick put his arm comfortingly around his daughter's
shoulders, kissing the top of her head as tears swam in his own
eyes. "It's alright, dear. He loved you, and he knew you loved
him. That's all that matters. That's all that ever mattered."

Standing there, consoling his daughter over his son's empty
grave, Urick felt like a fraud, an imposter. It should've been
him that sacrificed his life, Urick knew. **He** should be the one
floating in Temper's stomach right now, not Orion. A father's
sole purpose in life is to protect his family at all costs. Urick
had failed to do so, and Orion was dead now because of it. He had
paid the price.

Refusing to show the weakness inside of him for the sake of
his daughter, Urick hugged Maribel even tighter to his side, his
jaw clenched against the pain threatening to crush in on his
heart.

After a time of anguished silence filled with quiet tears,
Horris drew himself up to full height, took in a great breath of
air, wiped his wet nose on the back of his hand, and said, "The
lad wouldn't want it to be like this, us standin' around cryin'
and such...Common, we should give the others a hand rebuildin'."

Gently taking Maribel's hand, Horris turned and began leading
leading his crying niece through the steaming meadow of grass.
They hadn't gone far, though, when they realized Urick wasn't
with them. Conscerned, Horris turned back and said, "Urick, yeh
comin'?"

"Not yet." Urick's voice was low, his back turned as he
continued to stare regretfully at the small mound of stones at
his feet, an inadequate vestige to mark the life of a young man
as brave as Orion. He sighed. "You go on. I'll catch up."

Horris's eyes dropped as he somberly nodded his bald head.
He could not begin to imagine what his dear friend was going
through. Wordlessly, he hugged Maribel to his side like a doll as
they continued on towards the devastated village to salvage what
they could from the ruins.

Once they were gone Urick's watery eyes shifted to another
small mound of stones beside Orion's, this one partially
overgrown with green moss and yellowed lichens.

"Our baby boy's on his way home. I know you're going to love
seeing him again, Charlotte. He grew into such a fine young
man..." Urick's voice broke. Supressing a sob, he took in a deep
breath and tilted back his head, the tears he'd held restrained

finally streaming down his face. "I tried. I swear I did the best I could without you here."

The grave belonged to Charlotte, Urick's beloved wife, dead now for nearly ten years. She'd left early one morning to get the choice pick of the fisherman's catch when Temper had attacked the village. Urick never even had a chance to say goodbye. One moment she was there, and the next...gone, leaving Urick to raise their two small children by himself.

Perhaps it was Charlotte's abrupt disappearance, or the fact that he'd never had her body to lay to rest, but Urick's heart had never fully accepted Charlotte's death. Despite the strong urging of his friends and family, Urick had never taken another wife. Somehow, it just didn't feel right. He still loved her as if she were alive, still came to visit her grave and tell her about the milestones in their children's lives. To replace this part of his life with another woman would have felt like a betrayal.

And now, Orion had joined her, Temper having stolen them both from his life.

Sickened with heartbreak, Urick closed his eyes and prayed as he stood over the graves: If you've ever cared about anyone, God, you'll rid the world of this demon.

Then Urick turned and slowly began walking through the meadow towards the devastated village, the silvery morning mist swirling around him like so many lost dreams.

## CHAPTER 10

The massive team of black horses galloped down the narrow
mountain road, thundering iron-shod hooves ripping pits from the
ground as they pulled a covered wagon behind them. The driver of
the wagon was dressed in a hooded black cloak which flapped in
the wind rushing by him as he snapped the reins and yelled,
"Yaw!"

The horse-drawn wagon continued to speed through the tall
evergreens on the winding mountain road, dead leaves swirling in
its wake, wooden wheels rattling over the continuous thunder of
hooves.

The driver was leading the team of horses around a turn when
the densly packed forest abruptly opened up to a sprawling
meadow.

"Whoa now!" he called to the team of horses, hauling back

hard on the reins, "Whao! Whoa!"

As one the eight monstrous horses came to a halt, stamping and snorting and tossing their silky black manes.

The driver dropped the reins across his knees and reached up, pulling off the black hood which had concealed his face from view. He was a handsome young man, no older than thirty, with a strong jaw and an angular, chiseled face. His hair was the golden brown of wheat, long for a man, tied back from his face.

"No...," he said to himself, his cobalt-blue eyes scanning the distance ahead.

The modest, lake-side village before him lay in utter ruin. Rows of huts were leveled in piles of smouldering rubble, numerous ribbons of smoke rising from the ashes and slithering towards the broken clouds above. Sweaty, soot-covered men worked together in scattered groups, their laborous grunts of effort the only sounds they produced as they worked to clear the rubble. Women--some as filthy as the men--crouched amongst the ruins searching for what remained of their few possessions. Several of them were crying into their hands, having uncovered the lifeless bodies of their husbands or family members beneath the ruin. A group of grim-faced young men were lined in the meadow not far away, busy digging what appeared to be graves.

The stranger's blue eyes hardened with regret.

He'd come too late.

Sadly shaking his head, the stranger flicked the reins over the team of horses and drove his wagon towards the devastation.

CHAPTER 11

Urick and Horris stood in a long chain of sweating, filthy men, silently passing chunks of mud rubble down their line in a cimbined effort to help clear the devastation.

Both Urick and Horris had faired well this attack--in terms of property damages, anyway. Urick's home, located near the edge of the village, had gone entirely untouched by Temper's ruin, as had his smithy. Horris's hut had likewise been untouched, while his pub, located at the southern edge of the marketplace, had suffered only minor fire damage. Compared to the horrible losses of home and family many other villagers had suffered in Temper's attack, the brothers could have been called fortunate by some. But neither of them felt so, the loss of Orion hanging heavy in their hearts.

Side by side Urick and Horris continued to pass chunks of rubble down the line of grunting men as the clack of shovels, the

whinnying of horses, the pop-hiss of smouldering fires, and the
soft weeping of mourners continued all around them. Urick was
passing a blackened hunk of mud to Horris when he heard a man
further down the line say, "Now who the hell's that?"

Glancing up from their labors, the men saw a cloaked driver
sitting on the front of a large covered wagon, snapping a team of
massive black horses down the road through the meadow. As they
watched, the driver guided the team of horses into the village,
maneuvering the huge beasts through the smouldering piles of
rubble before coming to a stop.

Curious, dirty-faced children began to emerge from the
ruined village to gather in amazement around the team of giant
horses. Many other villagers took notice of the stranger as well,
glancing up from their labors to frown curiously. It wasn't often
travelers came to these parts, and the sight of such a fine wagon
and team of horses amid the destruction brought many odd stares.

"Who yeh think this might be, eh?" Horris asked, heaving
aside a boulder-sized chunk of rubble and slapping his hands
clean.

Urick's green eyes narrowed in his lined, dirty face,
sensing something odd about this stranger's sudden appearance to
the village.

"I don't know," Urick said, "But we should find out."

CHAPTER 12

The light-haired stranger reined the team of horses short,
bringing his wagon to a stop amid a swirling cloud of dust in the
center of the devastation. He then leaned forward and began tying
off the leads, noticing as he did so many villagers beginning to
emerge from out of the ruin, looking as dismal as ghosts with
their haggerd faces and filthy, ragged clothing. The sounds of
labor gradually diminished as men set aside their tools and women
collected their children. Cautiously, the villagers began
gathering around the team of massive black horses, all curious
to see who this stranger was.

One of the first to arrive was Urick, who crossed his arms
over his chest and asked, "Can we help you, sir?"

"You can," the stranger sitting atop the wagon said, his
voice holding a strange accent. "Please, tell me who governs this

land, and kindly point me in his direction. It is important that I speak with him immediately."

"This land is governed by no one," Urick explained, realizing the stranger was some sort of traveler unfamiliar with these parts. This struck Urick as odd, since all who dwelled in or even near this land lived in constant fear of Temper's wrath, never venturing further than necessary into the dragon's territory for fear of never returning. Surely this stranger had not ventured this far without having been warned of the dragon's presence dozens of times over. "This land is ruled by the dragon Temper. We no longer have a king. Whatever you need to say, you can say to us all."

The handsome stranger glanced around at the bedraggled villagers gathered around his wagon, all staring expectantly up at him. Speaking before large groups of people certainly wasn't the way he normally presented his services, but at the moment it didn't appear he had any other option.

"Very well." The stranger stood up atop his wagon and cleared his throat as he addressed the crowd of villagers surrounding him. "My name is Nethaneal Morris. I am a Dragon Slayer, come from afar to kill this beast called Temper."

If Nethaneal had expected a warm reception of praise and gratitude, as he had so many times in the past, he was sorely disappointed.

At his words the crowd of villagers simply began murmuring amongst themselves, fearing they'd heard the stranger wrong.

When Temper had first arrived in this land, he'd crushed an entire army of knights and ran king Warrington from his castle, claiming the territory and everyone who lived in it as his own. In all the years that had since passed, there had never been hope for Temper's defeat, only a bleak, fearfull acceptance of his dominion. A Dragon Slayer--especially one lone man such as the one standing before them now--was ludicrous. Absurd.

As the gathering of villagers continued to murmur in disbelief, Urick stepped forward and asked, "Have you ever **seen** Temper?"

Nethaneal frowned, not sure why that mattered. "Not, not directly. But I can assure you that won't--"

"Look around you," Urick suggested, his green eyes hardening. "Look at what he's done here. Temper is no ordinary dragon--this I can tell you from experience. All of us here can." Urick nodded his head towards the road leading out of the village. "I suggest you turn your team around and leave, Nethaneal. Perhaps you can still make it out of this land alive. We don't need another corpse to bury. We already have enough."

Urick then turned to leave and the rest of the villagers began to follow suit, the crowd dissipating back towards the devastation to return to their labors of clearing rubble and mending their homes, not even bothering to consider such a foolish notion. They had more important things to do than entertain this stranger's false hopes.

Realizing he was losing his audience due to their broken

spirits, Nethaneal cupped his hands around his mouth and called out to them, "Wait! All of you, please, wait! At least allow me to give you a demonstration of my weapon. It is unlike anything you have ever seen--this I assure you! If then you still doubt me, I shall turn around and leave at once!"

Intrigued by the proposition, the villagers paused and unsurely turned back, considering this stranger's words.

Urick turned back as well, a crease appearing on his sweaty, soot-blackened brow as he frowned. "What sort of weapon are you talking about?" he asked.

"Meet me in the meadow in one hour," Nethaneal said, glad to have won back the villagers' interest. "It is there that I'll show it to you."

CHAPTER 13

An hour later the crowd of villagers were gathered in the meadow, craning their necks to see past one another and murmuring amongst themselves as they waited for the Dragon Slayer's demonstration.

"Almost ready!" Nethaneal called out from behind his wagon parked in the grass a short distance away. This was followed by several laborous grunts and the sound of something very heavy being moved as he prepared for the demonstration.

As they waited, several men standing in the crowd shook their heads in angered disbelief, thinking it an utter waste of time to be standing there waiting for a demonstration from a man who clearly stood no chance against the likes of Temper. One of these men was Conner, who was pacing at the rear of the crowd with a contemptuous sneer on his gaunt face. He cared little for

the stranger's ridiculous demonstration, and was more concerned
with trying to find where Maribel was standing in the crowd.
**Where** was she?

A moment later Nethaneal appeared from around the side of
his wagon, bent over at the waist pushing a most peculiar-looking
contraption through the grass. It appeared to be a large iron
tube of some sort, as thick as a man's waist and nearly five feet
long. One end of the thick tube seemed bored hollow, while the
other was rounded and enclosed. And if that wasn't odd enough,
the curious iron tube was affixed to two large, wooden-spoked
wagon wheels which gave it a nearly comical appearance.

"The hell's that 'posed to be?" Horris demanded as the
stranger pushed the absurd contraption to a stop before them.
Others murmured their doubts as well.

Nethaneal straightened up and turned to the crowd of
villagers, dropping a long wooden pole and letting a leather
satchel slip off his shoulder with a heavy thud. "This, ladies
and gentlemen, is the newest weapon of modern warfare. It's known
as a cannon," Nethaneal explained, thoughtfully running his hand
along the cannon's black iron barrel as he walked around it. "For
too long our swords and arrows have proved ineffective against
most dragons. But no more. With this cannon, even a lone man such
as myself can face a beast like Temper--and walk away
victorious."

"Whatsit do?" a young boy at the front of the crowd asked.
His mother promptly pulled him back by the sleeve of his shirt
and hushed him quiet.

"Excellent question," Nethaneal said. He crouched down, rummaged in the satchel, and then stood up with a wool pouch resting in his outstretched palm. As the villagers' bewildered gazes tracked his movements, Nethaneal very carefully folded open the pouch to reveal a mound of some dark, granular substance inside. He offered it towards the gathering so that they could get a good look. Still unsure of the stranger and his odd contraptions, many of them shied away from his near presence.

"This is called black powder. Without it, this cannon would be a useless lump of iron. It's a brilliant mixture of saltpeter, sulfur, and charcoal. It was created by the people of China, who believed this powder to harness the very power of the dragon."

The gathering of villagers stared silently, their blank faces revealing their ignorance to all that had just been said.

"Right," Nethaneal pressed on. "Allow me to demonstrate how it works."

Moving around to the front of the cannon, Nethaneal stuffed the pouch of black powder into the barrel and picked up the wooden ramrod, using it to pack the cartridge down into the cannon. Once finished, he reached into his satchel and retrieved a heavy iron ball the size of a cantaloupe and held it up in both hands for everyone to see. "This is called a cannonball," he explained as he loaded it into the barrel. The heavy iron ball made a grinding noise as it rolled down the length of the barrel and knocked against something inside.

"The last thing that's needed is a spark," Nethaneal said.

He moved around to the rear of the cannon. There a thin serrated wire attached to a lanyard protruded from a narrow port at the cannon's bulbous end. Picking up the lanyard he said, "When I pull this wire, the friction will heat the primer, which will in turn ignite the powder inside. When this happens, there will be a very loud, powerful explosion. All of you will want to take a step back, and those of you with children will do well to cover their ears. Go on, make sure they're covered."

Upon Nethaneal's warning the crowd of villagers collectively took several unsure steps back, murmuring amongst themselves in bewilderment. Everything this stranger had just said to them had not made the least bit of sense, and none of them could guess what was about to happen.

Once the villagers were at a safe distance and the childrens' ears were covered, Nethaneal made final positioning adjustments to the cannon, aiming it at a gnarled oak tree standing in the meadow twenty paces ahead. Then Nethaneal stepped back and yelled, "Fire!" before jerking back on the lanyard.

The primer ignited as sparks fizzled down into the port...

...And for a delayed second, nothing happened.

Several of the villagers lowered their hands from their ears, glancing around in angry disappointment. Of course this man and his absurd contraption couldn't--

**BOOM!**

The cannon bucked as a gray cloud erupted from its barrel in a deafening explosion which echoed off the mountains, the

concussion flattening the grass ten feet in front of it. The
villagers gasped and jerked back, startled by the violent
explosion created by the strange contraption, their wide eyes
turning towards the oak tree.

The acrid smoke clearing on the gentle breeze, they saw that
a gaping, splintered hole was punched clear through the trunk so
that the swaying grass behind it could be seen. And as the
villagers watched, the tree let out a series of wooden groans as
it rocked backwards off its splintered stump and toppled into the
meadow with the crunch of snapping limbs.

For a long, breathless moment, nobody uttered a word.

"So...," Nethaneal said as he turned to the awe-struck
villagers, his keen blue eyes showing just a glint of humor at
their collective surprise, "Shall we discuss my fee?"

CHAPTER 14

"A **hundred** gold coins?" a bearded man roared, furiously
slamming his fist on the bar. "It's bloody robbery, 's'what it
is!"

After the shocking demonstration in the meadow, Nethaneal
had given them his price: One hundred gold coins in exchange for
killing Temper. The men of the village had promptly crowded
inside Horris's pub to discuss this, and as the sun began to set
they had so far come to no other agreement that their outrage at
the Dragon Slayer's preposterous demands. This particular
discussion was fastly becoming heated, the fear and frustration
of the last several days boiling over in a froth of agitation.

One sinewy man shook his fist in the air as the angered
cheers died out. "He might as well by that cursed dragon hisself,
come to steal what little we got left!"

"Not once in me life have I had ten gold coins to me name,
and he wants a **hunnerd**? Damn that basterd to hell fer his greed!"

"I say we run 'im off. Let the next town over pay to have
Temper killed."

"Fancy weapon or no, what's to stop him from makin' off with
our money once he gets it? How do we know this ain't no ruse?"

"That's right!" a surly-looking young man shouted as he
stood up with his fists balled, veins swelled in his neck. "If
the king's army couldn't kill Temper, he certainly can't. I say
he's a rotten swindler. I say we go and string him up!"

Their frustration and anger stoked into a rage, the men of
the village all cheered in murderous agreement as they worked
themselves into a frenzy.

"**ENOUGH!**" an angered voice suddenly boomed over the raucous
cheers and banging of fists on tables.

Startled into abrupt silence, the men all turned their
attention to the right, frowning at the interruption.

Across the smoky, lantern-lit pub Urick stood framed in the
dark doorway, his rigid face stony with anger, his green eyes
scowling at the congregation of men. He had been standing at the
rear of the crowd for the entire discussion, but had finally had
enough of their tongues. It was his turn to be heard.

"Listen to yourselves!" Urick accused them all with disgust,
his searing gaze scanning across the faces filling the pub as he
took several slow steps inside. "Listen to yourselves. This man
has come offering to kill Temper, and you want to run him off? To

string him up? You act as though he is our enemy and Temper is
our ally. Apparently I cannot speak for the rest of you, but I,
myself, would rather see Temper killed than this man."

"Now wait just a moment, Urick," an older man sitting across
the hazy pub interjected, angrily setting his pipe on the table
beside him. "You know right well none of us are on that dragon's
side. What we're sayin' here is that we can't afford no hundred
gold coins. Damn it, God knows we've already got it hard enough
tryin' to deal with the likes of Temper!"

The crowd of men filling the pub cheered their agreement,
glancing around and nodding their heads in support of one
another.

Urick waited until the cheers died out, then said, "Very
well. Then we will agree to pay his bounty, but only after he's
killed Temper. If he fails, we lose nothing."

"I doubt he will, but let's say he does kill Temper?" asked
a man standing with his elbows resting on the bar to face the
gathering. "How are we gonna pay him, huh? Didn't you hear? He
wants a hundred gold coins. A **hundred!** None of has that."

"Not one of us, no," Urick somberly agreed, turning in a
half-circle to meet the eyes of every man in the pub. "But if we
all give four of five coins, at the least, we can easily come up
with it."

"A man can feed his family for a year on that much alone,"
griped a man somewhere at the rear of the crowd.

"That you can," Urick agreed. "But what happens the next time Temper comes, huh? Or the next? Or the next? Some of you may not have a family left to feed. Think about that." Urick's stern eyes shifted to a man sitting at a table to his left. "John, would you spare the coins in your pocket to buy Angellica back?"

John's face flushed red at the mention of his dead daughter. "Damnit, you keep her name outta this, you rotten--"

Urick looked to another man. "Or you, Timothy? Would you spare your coins to buy back Gabriel? And what about you, Patrick? Would you give your coins to have Becky back? Gerrid? Would you pay to save Amy--"

**"STOP THIS!"** a heavy-set man barked before Urick could continue on with the long list of names of those killed by Temper. "For God's sake, we're all sorry that you lost your boy, we truly are. Orion was a fine good lad. And God knows we've missed Charlotte for years, the angel that she was. But this isn't helping matters none, and you know it."

"Isn't it?" Urick challenged the gathering of men. He was a hale man, and when angered he made for an imposing image in the center of the crowded pub. His jaw clenched bitterly, tears of pain swimming in his furious green eyes. "Temper has already taken my wife and my son from me. Those of you who haven't lost a loved one to Temper should cherish your luck. Because when it runs out--and it will--no amount of money will take their place. I would give my life ten times over to have my wife and son back. A handfull of coins is nothing to me. **Nothing.**"

Urick reached into his labor-worn trousers and tossed a
small cloth pouch onto the table with a metallic jangle. "Seven
gold coins. My entire savings," he said, "All that I have."

The pub was completely silent. Everyone knew Urick to be a
man as strong and unbending as the iron he hammered day in and
day out. If there was a man among them that truly labored for his
wages, it was Urick. And to have seen him give all that he had
while speaking from a place of such heartfelt sincerity struck a
chord deep within them all. They were all husbands and fathers
and brothers, after all, and they could only imagine what Urick
had been through. Perhaps he was right--it was worth any amount
of money to ensure their families' safety.

After a long silence Horris cursed, deciding to support his
brother no matter how much he doubted this Dragon Slayer. He
grabbed a mug sitting on the highest shelf behind the bar and
grudgingly dumped its contents on the counter. "Nine gold coins,"
he contributed. "Was gonna buy me some pigs fer the winter, but I
already got my hands full runnin' this sty."

The old man with the pipe sighed and leaned back, digging
into his vest pocket. "I got two. I'd wager the wife won't be
none pleased, but I suppose I can try to scratch up a few more."

"I've got four. Just sold me horse...," another man said.

None of the village men were wealthy, and although they
could ill afford to do so, one by one they took turns walking
forward and dropping their coins on the table. Urick had been
right, they all realized, their hard-earned gold nothing compared

to the love of their families.

Peeking through a crack in the far wall, Maribel watched from the darkness outside as the men added to the growing pile of coins on the table. Stepping away, she covered her mouth in disbelief.

Since the brutal defeat of king Warrington's army and the violent seizure of his lands, no one had dared oppose thee dragon's might. But they were going to do it. They were really going to pay the Dragon Slayer to kill Temper.

With hopeful tears welling in her eyes, Maribel turned away and hurried off into the village as the sun set beyond the lake in a blazing halo of crimson-streaked orange.

CHAPTER 15

The stars were just beginning to shine through the indigo-washed sky as the last crimson rays of daylight faded from the horizon. This scene was reflected double on the lake's surface, a watery mirror gleaming at the village edge. The nighttime insects were just beginning their light chorous of clicks, whirrs, and buzzes, while the frogs were well into their competing symphony of belches. The rich musk of earth was carried on the breeze sweeping off the lake, cool and gentle.

As the evening settled into night, Maribel left the ruined path of huts and began making her way through the meadow, her brown dress swishing gently amid the waist-high grass.

The Dragon Slayer had set up camp at the furthest end of the meadow away from the village. There he had erected a steepled canvas tent and parked his covered wagon nearby, the imposing

team of horses tethered in a row along its side. Sensing
Maribel's presence as she neared through the meadow, the horses
lifted their proud heads and nickered softly, tossing their silky
black manes.

Maribel stopped near the tent and smoothed the sides of her
dress before timidly calling out, "H-Hello? Is anyone in there?"

A light rustling came from within the tent, and then the
doorflap was folded open. "Yes?" Nethaneal asked as he ducked out
of the tent. He was wearing a dark pair of wool trousers and a
white shirt which hung loosely off his broad shoulders. His
golden, shoulder-length hair was tied back from his square face,
the soft glow of a burning lantern framing him in the tent's
doorway.

"I...I came to tell you that the men have agreed to your
bounty. One hundred gold coins," Maribel reported.

Nethaneal nodded. "Excellent. They will not be
disappointed," he promised.

"There's just one thing," Maribel began with a slight wince,
"They've collected the money and agreed to pay, but only once
Temper's been killed. We don't have much money, see, and everyone
fears that you'll...well...," she trailed off, looking down.

"Be killed?" Nethaneal finished, amusedly cocking an
eyebrow.

"Yes." The word must've escaped her lips without her full
permission, because Maribel's eyes widened and she was quick to
explain, "But it's nothing personal, I assure you! Many men

before you have tried to kill Temper, and all have failed. Most everyone seems to think you're either mad, or that you're a fraud."

"Which do you think I am?" Nethaneal inquired as he crossed his arms and leaned his shoulder against the tent's post, appearing slightly amused.

"Neither, I hope. But of all the men in the village, my father alone has faith in you, so I will trust his judgement."

"Yet you still don't seem convinced," Nethaneal observed.

"Not entirely," Maribel admitted. "It's just...my brother Orion was killed this last attack, and it's causing my father trouble. He's not the same, it seems. Neither of us are." She brushed a strand of hair out of her face and glanced away. "Orion died saving us."

Nethaneal studied Maribel's face in the grief-stricken silence that followed, watching as she fought back tears. His own eyes softened with compassion, gleaming sky-blue in the starlight. Deciding to change to a lighter subject, he said, "You mentioned that your father believed in me. Have I met him?"

"His name's Urick," Maribel said, wiping a finger beneath each of her eyes. "He's about your size, with dark hair. He--"

"Ah...The one with the black hands? Like a blacksmith's?" Nethaneal asked, recalling the stern man who'd confronted him when he'd first arrived to the village.

Maribel was startled by the Dragon Slayer's perception. "Yes, he is a blacksmith. How did you know that?"

Nethaneal shrugged. "I notice things. You have his eyes, you know."

Despite her earlier show of emotion, Maribel gave a reluctantly bashful smile and glanced away. Few ever took the time to notice, but Maribel felt that her eyes--very much her father's emerald shade of green--were her best quality.

Seeing that he had somewhat relieved Maribel's anxiety, Nethaneal pushed himself away from the tent's post and offered her his hand. "I don't believe we've been properly introduced. The name's Nethaneal Morris, at your service."

"Maribel O'hall," she said, taking his hand. Much to her surprise, Nethaneal bowed his head and placed a single kiss on the back of her hand.

"The pleasure's all mine, Maribel," Nethaneal said, straightening back up.

Maribel supressed a gasp and retracted her hand, shocked by the unexpected gesture. "Yes, well," she stammered, thankful for the evening shadows which concealed her burning face, "It's getting late. I should get back to the village. I just wanted you to know that the men have agreed to your price."

"Before you go, I was hoping you could help me," Nethaneal said, seemingly oblivious to the reaction he'd caused in her. "I've heard that Temper's lair is near in these parts. Would your father be willing to take me to see it tomorrow? From what you've said, I doubt anyone else will."

Maribel smiled faintly. "Of course. I'll ask him tonight

when I return."

"And Maribel? Just one last thing," Nethaneal added.

"Yes?" she asked, turning back.

"I want you to know that I will kill Temper, one way or another," Nethaneal said matter-of-factly, his blue eyes stern with sincerity. "You and your father won't have to live in fear any longer. I will set this right. I am no fraud, and I'm not entirely mad."

Not knowing quite what to say, Maribel simply nodded her head one sad, noncommital time before turning and walking away.

Nethaneal watched from the softly glowing doorway of his tent as Maribel faded into the darkness of the meadow, heading back towards her devastated village beneath a glittering dome of stars. The pity he felt for these poor people was trumped only by his hatred for Temper, a dragon which he'd yet to comfront, but somehow knew without a doubt he'd enjoy blowing ragged holes through. Once unable to see Maribel any longer, Nethaneal sighed and turned back into his tent, closing the canvas flap behind him to begin his studies of the region's maps. Now that the villagers had agreed to his bounty, he had much work to begin.

Not far away, peering through the darkness from around a tree at the edge of the forest, Conner narrowed his black eyes, his thin, angular face wrinkling into a malevolent scowl before fading back into the shadows.

CHAPTER 16

Conner ripped aside the doorflap of his hut and came storming inside, his labored breath hissing through bared teeth, his dark eyes blazing with anger.

Earlier Conner had followed Maribel from the cover of the forest as she'd made her way to the Dragon Slayer's tent, had crept forward and listened as best he could to their muffled conversation. Then he'd watched as the Dragon Slayer had bent down and kissed Maribel's hand--a gesture which had made hatred and jealousy boil like acid in the pit of Conner's stomach.

First that moron had had the nerve to drive his massive team of horses into the center of the ruined village as though he were royalty, proclaiming he was capable of slaying Temper in exchange for a ridiculous amount of money. And now he'd had the **audacity** to kiss Maribel's hand--a hand that Conner had for so long hoped to win in marriage.

Conner didn't know who this Nethaneal Morris thought he was, but Conner knew one thing for certain: Nethaneal would not take Maribel away from him. He would **not**.

"Idiot!" Conner spat, his thin body shaking with rage.

Conner wanted to confront Nethaneal and strike him down for touching his woman, but knew he would stand no chance in a physical confrontation against the muscular Dragon Slayer. Instead, Conner strode out through the rear of his hut to the stacks of rabbit cages lined outside. Still hissing curses in the darkness, Conner tore open one of the cages and reached inside, grabbing a brown rabbit by the soft scruff of its neck and wrenching it out.

Imagining the rabbit as Nethaneal, Conner sneered a leering grin and slowly began tightening his grip around the rabbit's neck.

The rabbit chittered softly and kicked its legs in the air, struggling feebly. Then its neck broke with a splintering snap, the animal's body going limp.

Disgusted, Conner flung the rabbit's lifeless body away and began to pace restlessly through the darkness, up and down the rows of stacked rabbit cages.

He'd only been there for a day, but Conner knew he had to get rid of the Dragon Slayer, one way or another. Grudgingly, Conner admitted to himself that he could not compete with the Dragon Slayer on many levels, all of which posed an immediate threat to his plans with Maribel. If she grew fond of Nethaneal--

the very thought curled Conner's stomach like sour milk--then he

would never again have a chance at winning her back. Conner loved

Maribel with every fiber of his being, loved her so badly he

sometimes felt his longing for her ache to the very core of his

bones. And he was sure Maribel loved him to, if not now, then

surely in the near future. Love like that wasn't accidental--they

were meant to be together.

Conner would be damned if the Dragon Slayer would ride into

the village on his fancy horses and strange weapon and steal

Maribel away from him. Conner would be **damned**.

But how, Conner wondered, would he manage to get rid of the

Dragon Slayer?

Conner continued to pace in the darkness, his mind racing

through the possibilities as he hissed nasty curses under his

breath. There had to be some way, some how...

The answer struck Conner like a bolt of lightning from a

cloudless sky, stopping him instantly in his tracks.

The idea was so extreme, so dangerous, so utterly mad, that

at first Conner was too frightened to even consider it. But then

he recalled the image seared into his mind of the Dragon Slayer

kissing Maribel's hand, and the surge of murderous jealousy

shattered his fear like a stone through glass.

Conner knew he had to do it. For Maribel, Conner would do

**anything**.

His dark eyes glimmering with anticipation in the silvery

starlight, Conner sneered and strode back into his hut to gather his things.

CHAPTER 17

"On a clear day, you can normally get a good view from up here," Urick said as he rode his horse up a grassy slope studded with gray boulders.

Following behind him Nethaneal rode atop one of his giant black horses, surveying the rolling green landscape around him as though shrewdly committing it to memory. A leather satchel was bundled on the rear of his saddle, his long woolen cloak swaying at his sides.

Straddling his downtrodden mare at the rear and looking entirely too large for the poor beast to carry, was Horris. Despite Urick's support of him, Horris still didn't trust the Dragon Slayer, and sat with his reins in hand, scowling up at the back of Nethaneal's blonde head of hair. Of course, it didn't help Horris's disposition any that Nethaneal's horse was so tall and broad that he had been forced to stare at its backside for the entire morning during their ride into the mountains.

One after the other the three men cantered their horses up the green hillside, cresting the ridge where a row of spindly oak trees stood trembling in the wind.

Urick stopped his horse and pointed into the distance ahead with a blackened hand. "There it is," he said, his eyes and voice flat with anger as he stared into the distance.

Nethaneal stopped his horse to the right of Urick, and Horris to the left. All three men sat in silence for a long moment at the top of the hill, squinting into the light breeze gusting up from below.

Before them the lush green forest of elders and evergreens rolled to the horizon, dotted here and there with grassy meadows and winding, silvery streams. Above, broken waves of clouds drifted lazilly across the brilliant blue sky. And in the distance far ahead, built atop a craggy ridge of mountains, was Temper's castle. From a distance the white stone fortress, with its towering spires and blocky stone ramports, loomed over the green lowlands like a godly palace, seeing and knowing all.

"**That's** Temper's lair, is it?" Nethaneal asked, sounding perplexed.

"It is," Urick confirmed. "After Temper slaughtered the king's army, he ran him from his castle and claimed it as his own." Urick turned his head to look at the Dragon Slayer. "You seem surprised."

"I am," Nethaneal admitted. "Dragons normally prefer caves or valleys as their lairs--they're secretive creatures, mostly.

It's not like most of them to choose such a conspicuous location to live."

Off to the side, Horris grunted and said, "Shows how much you know."

Ignoring his brother, Urick looked back at the castle perched in the distance, his face unreadable. "Does that matter, where he lives?" he asked.

"Most certainly. By studying a dragon's lair, you can learn much about it."

"Such as?" Urick asked.

"What's going on in its head, for one," Nethaneal said. "Think about the type of man who lives in a castle, as opposed to one who lives in a common hut. The man in the castle is often power-hungry, arrogant, and shrewd. This goes for dragons as well. They have personalities after all, just like we do. The fact that Temper would choose a castle as his lair--somewhere he'll be seen and known across the land--tells me he's jealous of his power. He thrives on the fear he instills."

Neither Urick or Horris commented on this. Nethaneal, despite having never encountered Temper, had just described the dragon in pinpoint detail. Perhaps the Dragon Slayer knew what he was doing after all.

After a thoughtful moment Nethaneal reached behind him and retrieved his satchel. From out of it he produced a quill and a sheet of parchment.

Horris leaned forward on his horse to look past Urick, frowning curiously at the Dragon Slayer. "What are yeh doin' now?" he asked.

Nethaneal dabbed the end of the quill against his tongue and flattened the wind-trembled parchment against his thigh as he began scribbling. "I'm taking notes," he explained without looking up. "I'm going to need to ask you two some questions, if that's alright."

"Anything," Urick said.

"How frequent are Temper's attacks?" was the Dragon Slayer's first question.

"Once a year, more or less." Urick shifted on the back of his horse, frowning. "There's many other villages he terrorizes besides ours."

Nethaneal made a quick note of this. "And what seems to be the dragon's preference?"

"How yeh mean?" Horris asked.

"Food," Nethaneal clarified. "What does he consume when he attacks the village?"

Urick's face soured as though a wave of nausea had hit him, the thought of Orion being referred to as food putting a knot of sickness deep in his stomach. "It seems mostly...humans," he finally answered.

Nethaneal's quill paused in mid-scrawl when he remembered that Urick had just lost his son only days earlier. Wishing he'd posed the last question a bit differently, he quickly moved on to his next question. "Has anyone ever attempted to flee the land?"

"Many have. But the terrain is rough in all directions but west." Urick nodded towards Temper's castle. "All roads lead past there. Everyone who's taken that route have been killed."

"I see." With that, Nethaneal rolled up the parchment and
stuffed it into his satchel. He then retrieved an odd contraption
that looked like a small wooden cylinder. He pulled one end of
it, and two additional segments--each smaller than the last--
extended outward with a series of clicks. Nethaneal then put the
narrow end of the contraption to his eye and pointed it towards
the castle, squinting through it.

Not knowing what sort of strange device the Dragon Slayer
was using, Urick and Horris exchanged an odd look. Horris
shrugged his broad shoulders in bewilderment.

As Nethaneal peered through the bleary orb of his telescope,
he carefully surveyed the exterior of the castle. Even from such
a far distance he could see that green ropes of ivy had begun to
snake up the outer stone walls. The massive iron gate in the
front entranceway seemed to have rusted halfway down from
closing. The windows in the top levels and spires were dark,
showing not a sign of life.

Nethaneal was studying the exterior of the castle when he
caught movement low on the telescope's round field of vision.
Shifting the telescope downward, Nethaneal saw something moving
behind the trees on the green hillside below the foot of the
castle.

At first it was only tiny shifts of hazy movement passing
between the columns of trees. But as Nethaneal tracked it, he
realized that whatever it was was traveling a long overgrown road

which led up the hillside towards the castle. The road sloped up
the hillside to the left, hooked back around, and led to the
castle's front gate. Nethaneal didn't get a good view of the
source of movement until it passed from the cover of trees and
began making its way across the two hundred yards of open ground
at the top of the ridge, headed for the castle: A rider sitting
on the front of a flat cart, being drawn by a single horse.

   Nethaneal leaned forward in his saddle and squinted into the
telescope, intrigued by what he was witnessing. Although the
image was blurry, Nethaneal could see that the driver of the cart
was a dark-haired man who looked to be rail-thin.

   Still squinting through the telescope, Nethaneal asked, "Do
either of you happen to know a skinny man, with dark hair? Drives
a flat cart?"

   Urick grunted knowingly as he sat on his horse, recalling
the last time Orion had ran Conner away from Maribel with a
glowing hot sword. "Name's Conner. He's a rabbit farmer, lives at
the end of the village. What about him?" he asked.

   "Nothing, really. Just wondering," Nethaneal said evasively.
Deciding to keep this odd development to himself, he lowered the
telescope from his eye and pushed it closed between his palms.
"Well, that's all I need for now, thanks. You two ready to get
back?"

   "Of course." Casting one last contemptuous look into the
distance at Temper's castle, Urick turned his horse away and
began cantering down the hillside to lead them back to the

village.

Nethaneal was hitching his tall black horse around to follow
when Horris said gruffly, "Yeh know what yer puttin' everyone
through, don't yeh?"

Nethaneal reined his horse short, turning back. "What do you
mean?" he asked, frowning.

"You know exactly what I mean." Horris turned his bald head
to make sure Urick was out of earshot before looking back at the
Dragon Slayer, his broad face simmering with restrained anger.
"Urick lost his boy four days ago, and couldn't even bury the
good lad 'cause he'd floatin' in Temper's belly. He had to raise
that boy an' his sister all by hisself, 'cause Temper ate his
wife some years back. I've know Urick since we were boys, an'
he's a strong man. But damnit, he can't take no more hurt, an' I
intend on seein' to it that none finds him.

"And now you show up, with yer fancy weapon, promisin' this
and promisin' that, getting folks' spirits up. Now I ain't
accusin' yeh of nothin', just so long as yeh mean what yeh say
and yeh follow through on it. Hell, I'll even spill my own blood
helpin' yeh kill that monster, if'n that's what it takes. But
know this: If what yer puttin' on is a ruse, hopin' to swindle
us outta our money, yeh best hope Temper gets to yeh first.
'Cause if not"--Horris fixed the Dragon Slayer with a deadly
stare he'd used to cower countless men, one that conveyed the
very real threat of danger--"I'll track yeh down, and I'll snap
yer neck with me bare hands."

Nethaneal studied Horris's ruddy face and stern brown eyes, and knew without question the large man was as loyal to his friends as a hound, and meant every word that he spoke. Despite the threat of injury, Nethaneal smiled pleasantly in return. "I like you, Horris," was all he said as he reached over and clapped Horris on the meaty shoulder before cantering down the hillside on his giant horse.

A scowl of angered skepticism on his ruddy, bearded face, Horris watched Nethaneal canter down the mountain. In all his life, no man had ever responded so casually to one of his threats. Something about the smug, self-confidant young man rubbed him the wrong way.

"Arrogant little shit," Horris growled, spurring his reluctant horse away.

Far in the distance, Temper's towering stone castle loomed like a deadly omen against the cloudy morning sky.

CHAPTER 18

"Silence!" Conner hissed at his mule, slapping the animal
hard across the snout. "Be quiet!"

Conner had parked his cart just yards from the castle's
towering outer wall. In response his mule brayed and bucked its
head, its eyes wide with fear and its nostrils flared as it
attempted to shy away. Even as dense and dimwitted a creature as
the mule was, it knew that a horrible presence lurked nearby,
could sense the death and evil on the air like static from a
coming storm.

"Worthless beast," Conner sneered, roughly tying its reins
around a boulder. Once the mule was secured, Conner picked up
three rabbit cages off his cart, one tucked under his left arm
and one in each hand, and began striding determinedly along the
side of the outer stone wall towards the front of the abandoned
castle. There the tall front gate stood halfway open like a

yawning mouth, green ropes of ivy draped from the sharp iron spearpoints like saliva from a monster's teeth.

Conner glanced back over his shoulder with dark, narrowed eyes, casting one last furtive look at the rolling lowlands below as the vague feeling that he was being watched crept upon him.

Realizing that it was of the utmost importance he go unnoticed for what he was planning to do, Conner had snuck from the village last night under the veil of darkness, not even lighting a lantern until he was well into the cover of forest. He'd traveled throughout the night and early morning to get to Temper's lair, never once seeing anyone on his backtrail.

Deciding it was simply his nerves beginning to tense, Conner shook off the feeling of being watched and ducked under the ivy-draped front gate, disappearing inside.

Within the castle's towering outer stone wall was what had once been a lavish, beautifully tended courtyard.

It now resembled an abandoned cemetery.

Through the years of neglect the courtyard had deteriorated into a ghostly, deserted sight. Waist-high weeds and spiny thistles choked the winding stone walkways. Rosebushes had either wilted to brittle sticks or spread into wild, overgrown tangles. Marble statues of saints stood like ghostly lepers, their sorrowful faces worn and disfigured by weather, green patches of moss, and bird droppings. Nearby a raven which had been perched on the edge of a stagnant, weather-cracked fountain cawed and took to the air. Then all was silent.

Cautiously, Conner waded through the weed-choked courtyard, his heart beginning to knock in his chest as he neared the looming castle. He was halfway across the courtyard when he kicked something hard laying hidden in the weeds. Glancing down, Conner saw what his boot had struck: A sun-bleached human skull, spindly clumps of weeds having sprouted up from its eyesockets, jagged nasal opening, and grinning mouth.

His stomach lurching with fear, Conner licked his dry lips and carefully stepped over the skull. Continuing on across the courtyard, he climbed the front steps one at a time and stopped at the castle's giant arched doors.

The doors were fifteen foot tall planks of wood banded together with thick slats of iron. The wood was splintered from exposure, the iron bands and door handles flaking with rust.

Before Conner attempted to open the door he tilted back his head and looked up at the castle to take in its full grandeur.

The enormous white stone castle stretched to the cloudy sky in fortressed levels, seeming to lean menacingly over him. The sharp points of the spires rose like the horns of a demonic God, the filth-blackened flags atop them whipping tatterdly in the gusting wind. The shattered windows were as staring and empty as soulless eyes. In the sky to the east, a smattering of clouds drifted past the late morning sun, casting a fluid shadow which passed ominously across the face of the deserted castle.

Just then the mule brayed from outside the walls.

Startled by the sudden noise, Conner jumped and jerked

around, dropping the cages at his feet. Inside the cages the
rabbits chittered and kicked their legs in agitation.

Realizing the sound had only been his mule tethered outside,
Conner cursed the mindless beast under his breath and ran his
fingers through his greasy black hair, discovering from the
dampness of his scalp that he had begun to sweat.

I'm doing this for Maribel, he reminded himself, to keep
that Dragon Slayer's filthy hands from ever touching her again.
For Maribel, I can do anything...

Embravened by this thought, Conner grabbed one of the door's
rusted handles and pulled. The tall door reluctantly inched open,
the rusted hinges moaning like the waking dead. Then, gathering
up his rabbit cages and taking one last deep breath to steady his
humming nerves, Conner stepped inside the castle.

The damp smell of mold, decay, and long-settled dust
assaulted Conner's nostrils before his eyes could adjust to the
darkness. Then his surroundings gradually came into view: He was
standing in the doorway of the castle's foyer, a sprawling
expanse entirely devoid of life. A decade's worth of dirt and
grime coated the sprawling marble floors. Cobwebs were draped
like lace from the arm of an ornately carved statue in the
corner. Through a shattered window nearby, searching ropes of ivy
had snaked through, a drift of dead leaves which had blown in
scattered across the floor.

His rabbits beginning to chitter and rustle nervously in
their cages, Conner slowly began making his way across the

massive foyer, his bootheels echoing hollowly on the grimy marble
floor.

On either side of the foyer stone walls stretched up to the
cavernous, arched ceiling fifty feet above. There a massive
chandelier hung, surely once beautiful, but now draped with
cobwebs and adorned with small black bats which squeaked and
chattered their sharp little teeth as Conner passed below. On
the wall a portrait of a forgotten king stared out from behind an
obscuring layer of dust and mold, its hazy eyes ghostly and
watchful in the absolute silence of the castle.

The foyer opened up to a massive grand hall where jeweled
daylight slanted down in dusty columns from the steepled,
stained-glass windows to the left of the hall. Ahead, two
sweeping flights of marble stairs descended from the second level
of the castle.

As he surveyed the sprawling, empty hall before him, Conner
watched as a rat scurried noiselessly across the floor ahead,
passing through the jeweled patterns of light and skittering
beneath an overturned table. Somewhere, unseen but not far away,
the feathered beat of wings sounded as a pigeon took to the air.

Conner used his shoulder to wipe the moisture from his top
lip as he tried to decide which way to go. Continue forward, or
try one of the flights of stairs? Where in the castle would a
dragon such as Temper make his lair? he wondered.

As Conner was struggling to make up his mind another cloud
drifted across the face of the sun outside, for the jeweled

columns of light cascading down from the stained-glass windows
suddenly dimmed, casting the castle's vast, lifeless interior
into shadows. Far down one of the distant corridors the wind
moaned through a shattered window, echoing like a lost soul. A
hinge creaked.

Conner shivered.

Fearfully, Conner decided to try the stairs to the left. He
made his way across the grand hall, past rotting, overturned
furniture and a rusted suit of armor which had collapsed to the
floor and become a shelter for rats. He arrived at the base of
the stairs and began up the long, curving ascent, wincing as the
sound of his boots striking the marble was amplified a dozen time
times over in the vast, silent castle. Finally coming to the top
of the flight of stairs, Conner took in a silent breath and held
it, trepidation cementing his feet to the floor.

Ahead of him, a tall arched doorway stood open, From the
angle that Conner stood, he could only see one rough stone wall
and a single marble pillar, nothing which should have pierced him
with such an icy lance of fear that now seized his body. Temper
was in there; Conner could **feel** the dragon's daunting presence
from around the corner like a low hum of electricity flowing
across his nerves. In their cages the rabbits were completely
silent, huddled fearfully against the back of their cages,
shivering with terror.

Instinctual fear screaming in his ears, Conner was seriously
considering turning back when a voice so powerful that it sent

tremors throughout the castle said, "I smell you there, human...
Come forward. It will do you no good to turn back now."

Conner's throat was so dry that it clicked as he swallowed,
his trembling legs obediently walking forward as if on their own
accord. Timidly stepping into the doorway, Conner saw a massive
chamber stretching before him. Each side of the hall was lined
with a succession of tall marble pillars, ending at a sprawling
expanse which could have only been the king's quarters.
Magnificent stained-glass windows rose to towering heights
against the back wall, imposing scenes of battle and glory which
shone like jewels in the sunlight. And sprawled on the floor just
below them was a brooding silhouette, so large it nearly filled
the quarters--Temper, his massive, scaled body coiled on a
glimmering bed of gold and jewels.

"I...I only come in your honor, m-mighty Temper," Conner
stammered as he forced his legs to carry him down the length of
the hall.

Temper stirred, lifting his fearsomely horned head thirty
feet into the air, casting an imposing shadow over Conner.
Outside the cloud which had passed before the sun moved on,
revealing the dragon's horrid features: Razor-sharp teeth bared
in a serpent-shaped head; plated jade scales bristling; ruby-red
eyes glowing maliciously in the dim light.

"My honor, you say," Temper mused, considering the scrawny
human standing before him. "I need not the honor of a mere human.
I already hold the fear of all in this land. It is mine, as is

all who dwell here."

Conner dropped his eyes, unable to hold the dragon's cowering gaze for long. "Of course, mighty T-Temper. You do not need anything from me. But I have come to promise my loyalty to you and...and to offer my gifts."

"Gifts?" Temper narrowed his blood-red eyes in suspicion of the human. "What gifts do you have to offer me, with all that I already possess?"

A nervous smile twitching one corner of his thin lips, Conner set the rabbit cages down and slid them one by one across the marble floor towards Temper. "I have brought you these from my stock, all that I could carry. A humble gift, I know, but I would be honored if you would accept my offerings," he explained, clasping his hands behind his back to hide their trembling.

"I see..." Reaching forward, Temper shattered one of the cages, and with his sharp, hooked talons plucked out one of the squabbling, kicking rabbits. Lifting the creature in the air, the monstrous dragon dropped the rabbit into his open mouth and ended its life with a small, muffled crunch. Temper then slid a black forked tongue across his scaled lips and said, "A mere morcel to whet my appetite. Now, if you have nothing more to offer me, I shall desire something a bit more...**flavorfull**." And Temper began to lower his head towards Conner.

A look of horror crossed Conner's pale face as he held up both hands, Temper's fearsome head looming over him. "Wait, mighty Temper! Gifts are not all that I have come bearing!"

Temper paused, his slitted red eyes narrowing skeptically down at the trembling human who'd dared disturb his rest. "What else do you have for me?" he demanded.

Conner looked as though he were about to vomit. "I've come to tell you that a man, c-claiming to be a Dragon Slayer, has come to our village. He has offered to kill you for a hundred gold pieces. The word is that the villagers are willing to pay."

Temper raised back his head and snorted two bursts of steam in disgust. "Ridiculous. Entire legions of knights have come before me, and all have failed. One man is nothing to me."

"Certainly, mighty Temper," Conner began tentatively, "It's just that, this man has--"

"Has **what**?" Temper demanded angrily, lowering his head down to Conner and menacingly revealing his teeth, some of which were the length of a man's forearm.

Conner squeezed his eyes shut and braced himself, forcing his trembling legs not to give way beneath him. He could smell the dragon's searing hot breath washing over him, the odor of death and hunger. "He, he has a weapon, mighty Temper, like none I've ever seen before. A cannon, he calls it. A most strange devise. P-Powerful enough to topple a tree with one blow."

"No weapon created by man can harm me!" Temper snarled, his breath so hot that it shimmered the air.

"Of course, great Temper. I merely thought it wise to inform you that as we speak, the villagers are planning a mutiny. All but me, that is," Conner explained servilly.

Temper's horned head cocked shrewdly, his sharp talons

tapping thoughtfully on the cold marble floor. "And why is it you felt the need to tell me this, human? And do not lie. I'll smell it on your flesh."

"A woman," Conner admitted, knowing better than to lie to the murderous dragon before him. "I love her, and this Dragon Slayer, Nethaneal Morris, threatens our relationship together." Conner's eyes turned cold as he looked up at Temper. "I came here to tell you this, so that you may kill him and all the others who've put their trust in him. I want her all to myself."

Temper slowly bared his sharp teeth in a vicious, reptiallian grin. He could smell the raw hatred, the betrayal, and the murderous intent wafting off the human's skin like poison, and was impressed. Perhaps he wouldn't kill this particular human after all, the kindred, of not inferior, soul that he was. Besides, Temper reconsidered with cold calculation, it would be much more amusing to learn through this human how hopeful the villagers were to be rid of him, and then how devastated they are when he slaughtered this Dragon Slayer and then makes another feast of their village for their sedition.

"Very well," Temper conceded, batting his forepaw dismissively to the side, "I shall let you live. And in return, you will keep me informed of this Dragon Slayer and all who support him. They will be punished."

A triumphant grin spreading slowly across his gaunt face as he stared up at the monstrous dragon, Conner replied unctuously, "Yes...anything for you, **mighty Temper.**"

CHAPTER 19

Later that afternoon the villagers were hard at work clearing away what was left of Temper's ruin. Chains of grunting, filthy men passed heavy chunks of rubble along their lines to be stacked on carts and hauled away. Horses whinnied at the sharp crack of reins and surged forward, toppling charred remnants of huts and shops and dragging them away. Women carried buckets of lake water, while the young and elderly provided what foodscraps they could gather for the workers. This was not the first time that Temper had spread his wrath here, and as a village they knew they had to come together to repair what had been lost.

As the villagers' laborous activity continued all around him, Nethaneal strolled down what had once been the market's lane, closely studying the damage. Just like when tracking an animal through the forest, Nethaneal had found from experience that he could learn much about a dragon simply by visiting the scene of its last attack.

One of the first things to catch Nethaneal's attention was the skeletal remains of a burnt wooden cart. Crouching down beside it, Nethaneal brushed a blonde strand of hair out of his face, his keen blue eyes examining the angles of charred wood. After a moment of studying it, he rapped his knuckles against the cart's siding. The wood, as charred and brittle as charcoal, promptly cracked and fell in on itself, blackened chunks sprinkling to the ground.

Sifting his fingers through the ashes, Nethaneal uncovered one of the nails which had held the cart together, raising it to his face for examination.

The short iron spike was twisted and warped, nearly into the shape of an S.

Nethaneal frowned. The heat required to warp iron was awesome--even by the fierce standards of dragon fire.

Tossing the nail aside and slapping the soot from his hands, Nethaneal stood and continued to follow Temper's path of destruction through the village.

As he strolled past the groups of laborers Nethaneal found it odd that the dragon had descended solely on the marketplace, leaving the majority of the outlying huts in the village entirely untouched. There would be more people there during the day, sure. But why not target the cattle at the north end of the meadow? Or the pigsties? Or the horse stables? All of those would have been much larger meals requiring only half the effort.

Again, Nethaneal found this detail odd.

He continued to stroll through the devastated village with his hands in his pockets, thoughtfully mulling over the implications of the things he saw around him.

Just then a cool breeze gusted off the lake and over the village, swirling the black ashes over the ground and stirring the smell of charred thatch on the air. In the cloudy sky above a ragged white tuft gracefully slid across the sun's face, dimming the afternoon sunlight.

Instantly all sounds of labor throughout the village ceased. Sweating workers, women, and even young children all stopped what they were doing, fearfull eyes frantically searching the sky above them for danger.

Unaware of its impact, the cloud continued drifting by on its slow current, the sun's rays brightening once more.

The villagers' collective sigh of relief was nearly audible as they resumed their individual activities, thankfully shaking their heads that it hadn't been Temper which had blocked out the sun.

Nethaneal, who'd looked up just in time to notice the villagers' reaction to the dimming sunlight, made a mental note of this as well. In all of his travels, he doubted he'd ever encountered this level of fear instilled by any one dragon. And that said something, considering the ferocity of several of the dragons he'd slain in the past. Whatever breed Temper was, he was obviously no ordinary dragon to have cowered these poor people into a state of such paranoia.

With a renewed sense of determination for the sake of the

villagers, Nethaneal continued scouting the dragon's path of
destruction through the center of the village, noticing details
here and there which he shrewdly catalogued and stored away in
his mind.

One of the things he noticed was the charred remains of an
ox whose body, from the shoulder blades back, was missing,
blackened entrails spilling from its chest cavity. Nethaneal
waved away a cloud of flies to inspect the rotting ox carcass,
wincing at the stench.

The wound had been delivered by wide, serrated teeth which
had cut through hide, flesh, tendon, and thick bones in one
savage bite. The spacing of the teeth, Nethaneal judged from the
wound, was approximately six inches from point to point--which
meant teeth roughly the size of shovel heads.

Still crouched down, Nethaneal reached into the satchel
hanging off his shoulder and retrieved a quill and parchment,
taking a moment to scribble down the list of details he'd
observed. He was just finishing when a timid female voice asked,
"Pardon me, sir, but...aren't you the Dragon Slayer?"

Nethaneal looked up from his notes to see a rather worn-
looking woman standing to his right. She appeared to be in her
thirties, with mousy brown hair, a tired face, and a threadbare
dress blotched with numerous stains.

Rolling up the parchment and returning it into the satchel,
Nethaneal answered as he stood up, "I am. The name's Nethaneal
Morris."

"Nethaneal," the woman said with a smile. It was an attempt to be pleasant, but the gesture only revealed more of the pained worry already apparent on her lined face. "My name's Rebecca. I've--I've come to ask if you could help my husband, Stephen. I know you're busy, surely, and I hate to bother you, but if you could come and take a look at him, we would be indebted. He was bitten by Temper, and he is not at all well. I suppose it's a miracle he's still alive at all--a true sign from the Gods that he isn't yet to die. He'll pull through, I'm sure of it--"

"I'd be happy to, Rebecca," Nethaneal politely interrupted the woman, for she had begun to ramble. Besides helping the woman's injured husband, Nethaneal could use this chance to gain more information concerning Temper.

Rebecca smiled and touched the base of her neck, so thankful that it appeared she might break down into tears. Instead, she replied, "He's not far, Stephen. I'll take you to him."

Following Rebecca through the devastation, Nethaneal was all too aware of the conversations becoming hushed as he walked by. Men paused in the midst of their labors to glare suspiciously at him, while women and girls covered their mouths to whisper secretly amongst themselves in small huddled groups. Nethaneal knew the varied effects that his good looks and conspicuous presence as a Dragon Slayer had on the villagers, both men and women alike, yet paid them no mind. He was here to kill Temper and free them from the dragon's terrors. Nothing more.

"Right over here," Rebecca said over her shoulder, turning down a narrow dirt lane and leading Nethaneal to a small hut at the edge of the village. She pulled the doorflap aside and invited him in with a polite sweep of her hand. "Please, come in," she offered, still with her strained smile.

Ducking through the low doorway, the first thing Nethaneal noticed as he came into the hut was the horrendous smell: The pungent odor of sweat-dampened skin mixed with a noxious, sickening stench of rot.

"This is Stephen," Rebecca said, brushing past Nethaneal and hurrying across the hut's cramped, dirt-floored interior. There she kneeled down beside a man laying face-up in a cot, sliding a hand comfortingly over his dark, messed hair. "Stephen," she whispered near his ear, speaking in gentle tones, "I found someone that can help you. Stephen? Stephen, I brought him here. He's a Dragon Slayer."

Nethaneal walked over and stood next to Rebecca at her husband's side. The man was laying on his back, a wool blanket pulled up to his chin soiled with what appeared to be dried vomit. The man's face was as pale as a corpse's. A feverish sweat glistened off his forehead, beads of sweat rolling from his face and darkening the blanket folded beneath his head.

"Stephen, can you hear me?" Rebecca asked, an anguished tremor in her words.

With what appeared to take immense effort, Stephen's sunken eyelids wavered open just enough for his glossy, yellowed eyes to drift lazily towards his wife. Then he groaned miserably, his eyelids drifting shut.

Rebecca took one of her hands away and pressed it to her mouth to suppress a sob.

"Where was he bitten?" Nethaneal asked, hoping to keep the poor woman brom breaking down.

"His leg, nearest you," Rebecca said through her fingers splayed before her mouth. "He was trying to save our only horse when that damned..." Unable to say more, she returned to petting her husband's hair, her tear-filled eyes searching his face for signs of improvement.

Rolling up the sleeves of his cloak, Nethaneal crouched down on one knee and began toppull the wool blanket back to inspect the man's wounds. But he quickly discovered that the blanket had fused to the fluids of the wounds concealed beneath it, forcing him to slowly **peel** it away from the man's flesh.

Stephen turned his head and moaned weakly against the pain of his disturbed wound. Rebecca cupped his glistening face in her hands and continued to whisper comfort to him as the Dragon Slayer inspected his leg.

Nethaneal grit his teeth as Stephen's wounds were revealed from under the soiled blanket, bracing himself against the awful sight and even worse smell.

Stephen's leg no longer resembled a human limb. The leg was so swollen and misshapen that the skin covering it--now dark green laced with a network of blackened veins--had taken on a smooth, taunt surface. A row of large punctures left by Temper's fangs were ringed with dead flesh, thick brown puss weeping continuously from each of the wounds.

Having seen enough, Nethaneal lowered the blanket to cover Stephen's leg, feeling hot bile rise in his throat as the rancid stink of the infection wafted past his face.

"What do you make of it? Can you help him?" Rebecca worried, still smoothing her husband's hair. She seemed oblivious to the stench filling the cramped hut.

"There is one thing that will ease his suffering. But you won't like it," Nethaneal said as he remained kneeling beside the cot, sadly meeting the woman's gaze.

"What? What is it?" she asked pleadingly, urgency quickening her words. "I'll do anything."

"Go out into the forest. Gather together as much nightshade as you can find. Brew it into a warm tea"--Nethaneal turned his eyes regretfully down to Stephen's feverishly pale face--"and give it to him to drink."

"But...nightshade, that will kill him," Rebecca said, her brow wrinkling incredulously.

"Exactly," Nethaneal affirmed. He explained: "There is venom in Temper's bite. When you husband was bitten, it got into his body. Now that venom is flowing through his veins. It will continue to destroy his body, little by little, causing him unbelievable pain. Soon, you will not even recognize him. The venom will travel up his body to his brain, and then he will become delirious--mad. He will die a terrible death, screaming with agony, until his innards break down into liquid." Nethaneal looked Rebecca straight into her wide, teary eyes and said with

regretful honesty, "There is no remedy for dragon's venom. It is
the cruelest of any. If you love this man, which I believe you
do, very much so, then you will end it for him quickly. It will
be the best way, for the both of you."

Rebecca's eyes became unfocused with shock as the
consequences of the Dragon Slayer's words set in. She opened her
mouth as if to speak, but let out a cry and broke down into tears
as she clutched her dying husband's head in her arms.

Quietly offering his condolences to the sobbing woman,
Nethaneal stood and left the hut. Once in the fresh air outside
he stopped near the street and wiped his hand down his face,
thinking to himself as he watched the villagers pass by,
attending to their labors amongst the scarred village.

The size of Temper, the heat of his flame, his ferocity,
his venemous bite...None of it made any sense.

**What** kind of dragon was he dealing with here?

Nethaneal was pondering this when he happened to notice,
from between two huts and out across the meadow, a horse and cart
emerge from the treeline and start towards the village.

Nethaneal's eyes narrowed alertly. Instantly recognizing the
thin, dark-haired driver of the cart--Conner, his name was--as
the one he'd seen disappearing into Temper's castle earlier that
morning, Nethaneal took a quick step sideways to conceal himself
behind a tall stack of hay, his sharp blue eyes peering
watchfully through the tangled brown stalks.

Conner drove his cart along the dirt road, passing by only

yards away with the rickety creak of wooden wheels. And as he did
so, Nethaneal caught the look on Conner's pale, angular face as
he sat atop the cart's bench: Happiness, at first glance, but
mixed with something much more sinister, something which turned
Conner's thin smile into a cold sneer of triumph and sapped the
life from his dark eyes. Then he had passed by, driving his cart
back into the village.

Intrigued, Nethaneal plucked a straw of hay from the pile
beside him and thoughtfully chewed its end for a moment, turning
this peculiar development over in his mind, examining it from all
angles, calculating what exactly could be done with it. There
were only so many reasons a man would go to the lair of a dragon
as fierce as Temper--not one of them pleasant. And the fact that
Conner had returned unscathed and in such apparent secrecy spoke
volumes. So what had he been doing there?

After a moment Nethaneal tilted back his head, judging from
the sun's position low in the west that nightfall was not far
off. Logging this bit of information away, Nethaneal plucked the
straw of hay from his mouth and tossed it aside as he strode off
into the village to return to his tent.

He had much to ponder.

CHAPTER 20

The following morning a row of women were crouched down at
the lake's edge, busy washing clothes and gossiping amongst
themselves as the rebuilding efforts began in the village.

"I'm telling you, if I wasn't already married to Thomas...,"
a young, red-haired woman said, trailing off with a sigh.

The older woman beside her laughed and shook her head as she
scrubbed a pair of trousers. "And that's what to stop you? If I
was your age again, I'd have bed him twice already, husband or
no."

"That's no surprise," a third woman commented, looking over
with mischievous eyes, "Since it's been years the last time your
husband shared your bed?"

"Months, I'll remind you," the older woman bristled.

"I don't care what any of you say," the woman at the end

said, scrubbing a blouse against a rock as she looked out over
the water. "If he looks at me twice I'm going to wrap myself
around him like bark on a tree."

"Annett!" the women all gasped before breaking into
laughter.

The object of their attention was Nethaneal. The Dragon
Slayer was fifty yards down the lake shore bathing in the waist-
deep water with his shirt off. As the group of women watched
discretely, Nethaneal cupped his hands in the water and splashed
it on his face, the sun's early rays glistening off his heavily
muscled shoulders, chest, and stomach.

The row of women were still commenting on their salacious
intentions with the handsome young man when Maribel arrived with
a basket of clothes tucked at her side.

"Good morning, ladies," she greeted, taking her place beside
them on the rocky lake shore.

Knowing Maribel had just lost her twin brother a week prior,
the women immediately cut their colorful conversation short.

"Good morning to you, Maribel," the oldest of the women
said gently. "How are you today, dear?"

Maribel lifted a pair of her father's trousers out of the
basket and shrugged good-naturedly as she submerged them in the
lake water. "Fine, I suppose. Thank you for asking."

"And your father? How is he?" the red-haired woman asked,
looking concerned.

"He's just fine. Staying busy," Maribel assured her.

This, of course, was something of a lie. Ever since Orion's death her father had been spending the days in the confines of the smithy. From sunup until sundown he would hammer hot iron, coming home late at night looking horribly exhausted and leaving again before sunup the next day. Perhaps it was just his way of grieving, Maribel had considered, but still she worried over her father.

"That's good, dear," the older woman said. She smiled as she turned back to scrubbing her clothes, deciding to try and brighten Maribel's day. "You came just in time, you know."

"Just in time for what?" Maribel asked, taking the bait.

"Right over there," the woman closest Maribel leaned over and whispered, nodding her head down the lake shore.

Maribel looked, her green eyes widening.

Half-naked, the Dragon Slayer was ringing lake water from his long golden hair, his arms bulging with muscle in the crisp morning air, the sunlight sparkling off the disturbed water all around him.

"We heard you visited his tent," the older woman said, arching a single eyebrow conspiratorily.

"Yes--what was he like? A gentleman?" one woman asked eagerly.

"Not too gentle a man, I'd hope," another commented.

Feeling her face burn with embarrassment, Maribel tore her eyes from Nethaneal's sculptured body and shook her head as she resumed scrubbing clothes with new vigor. "We spoke a bit about

his agreement to slay Temper. That was all," she explained, not
quite knowing why she felt so defensive. Perhaps it was because
she had found herself attracted to Nethaneal, but considering
that she'd just lost her brother she didn't feel it was an
appropriate time for such things. Besides, her father needed her
right now, more than ever. She hadn't the time to be courting
men, especially a Dragon Slayer such as Nethaneal.

"Mm-hmm," the eldest woman responded with a critical eye,
ringing out a shirt and tossing it in a basket. "You're of the
age where a woman needs a man, Maribel. Keep that in mind. And
that man there is one fine specimen, whether he can kill dragons
or not,"

"Indeed," the red-haired woman agreed, still staring down
the shoreline. The shirt she had was clean, yet still she
continued to scrub it.

Ever since she'd lost her mother as a child, Maribel had
valued the advice of these women concerning the feminine matters
her father was unable or unwilling to provide. Right now,
however, she wished they'd keep their comments to themselves.
It was embarrasing.

"I'll find a man in my own due time, thank you very much,"
Maribel snapped, hurrying to ring out the last of her clothes
before she'd even finished scrubbing them properly. She tossed
them together into the basket and stood up with it under her arm.
"And when I do, I'll thank you all to keep your lecherous eyes
off of him!" Then she turned and walked quickly away in

exasperation.

The eldest woman smiled wisely as she continued to scrub clothes at the lake's edge and said, "The poor girl's already smitten."

The rest of the women all agreed as they continued to ogle the Dragon Slayer, looking quite smitten themselves.

CHAPTER 21

A sharp scowl on his bony, pale face, Conner advanced
through the village at a brooding, unhurried walk.

All around him the villagers were hard at work in the warm
afternoon sun. Horses pulled cartloads of hay, chains of sweating
men stacked mud bricks, and ropes snapped taunt to raise wooden
beams. Workers yelled to one another over the sounds of labor, as
did several of the vendors who'd already rebuilt their shops and
were once again hard at work peddling their wares, the aroma of
baking bread, wood fires, and cooking meat drifting on the air.

With the rubble and ruin of Temper's last attack cleared
away, the villagers had now begun the arduous process of
rebuilding. And with it had come an atmosphere of positive
communal effort. Instead of sifting through the ashes and
mourning their losses, the villagers were now helping one another

build anew, the labor lifting the spirits of all in the village.
For the first time in many days there was laughter from the
children and smiles from the workers as they began putting
Temper's horrible attack behind them.

Conner could not have cared less. As he slowly advanced
through the village he paid no mind to those around him, his
dark, glaring eyes focused intently in front of him.

There, twenty yards ahead, Maribel was strolling through
the village, occasionally smiling and waving to those she
passed. Her long dark hair was braided back into a tail, and she
was wearing a faded brown dress with a basket of potatoes hooked
in the bend of her arm.

Conner clenched his small, plaque-rimmed teeth in anger as
he tracked Maribel's path through the village like a hungry puma
in the forest.

Ever since the Dragon Slayer's arrival, Conner had found
himself obsessed with following Maribel's every move throughout
the day, neglecting his rabbits, sometimes going without food and
water for long periods. It was as if by keeping her within his
sight that Conner hoped to keep Maribel away from Nethaneal,
hoped to maintain the bond between him and her.

Of course, this hadn't worked.

On several different occasions Conner had spotted Maribel
speaking with the Dragon Slayer throughout the village, lavishing
him with attention. And each time Conner had felt mounting hatred
for the Dragon Slayer pumping through his veins, a jealous rage

burning in the pit of his stomach as he crouched in his hiding spots, watching them together with black, narrowed eyes.

Nethaneal had rode into the village, full of pompous grandeur, and Maribel had been foolish enough to fall for the Dragon Slayer's act. The stupid, foolish girl.

The only consolation that Conner felt from all of this was knowing that soon, when the time was right, Temper would rip the Dragon Slayer to mangled shreds and feast on the corpses of all who'd instilled their trust in him. Then, and only then, could Conner reveal to Maribel that he had stood before the mighty dragon Temper and lived to tell about it--using not a single weapon, but rather his mind, his superior intelligence, to gain the dragon's favor. And with it, Maribel would see that it was Conner, and Conner alone, that truly loved her and could protect her from the dragon's wrath. Then she would be his, at long last.

In the market not far ahead Maribel stopped and began speaking with an elderly merchant in his newly rebuilt shop, smiling pleasantly and laughing.

Immediately Conner stopped and turned his face away, pretending to find interest in a table stacked full of leafy green vegetables.

As Conner secretly watched Maribel from the corner of his eye, a portly woman with blonde hair stood up from behind the table and said kindly, "Afternoon, young man. What can I get you? I've got carrots, beets, peas-"

"Nothing. Be quiet," Conner snapped as he craned his neck

distractedly to the side, watching Maribel say goodbye to the shopkeeper and continue on into the marketplace.

The portly woman standing across the table gave a look of shock, then anger at the young man's insolence, and was beginning a retort when Conner turned away and once again began following Maribel through the market.

Maribel had just turned down a side alley, making her way towards home, when she felt a hand grab her roughly by the shoulder. Letting out a startled gasp and spilling several potatoes from her basket, Maribel turned and saw Conner standing directly behind her.

"Conner! I told you not to do that anymore! What are you thinking?" she demanded, angrily stooping low to gather the potatoes off the ground.

Conner scowled like a petulant child as he stood looking down at her, his black, middle-parted hair glistening with oil in the sunlight. "I should ask you that same question!" he said, angrily spitting out the words like an accusation.

Collecting the last of the potatoes, Maribel stood and took a cautious step back to put some distance between them. "What do you mean by that?" she asked, confounded by his sudden anger.

Conner's dark eyes hardened to stone in his pale face. "You know exactly what I mean, **Maribel**! You and that...that **Dragon Slayer**. I've seen you two together. Don't try and deny it." Conner took another quick step forward, closing the space between them to inches. "He is not as great as he claims, Maribel. Temper

will kill him, I assure you of this. And once he is dead, I will
be the only one that can protect you."

Maribel held the basket of potatoes up to her chest as
though hoping it would ward Conner off. "What are you talking
about, Conner?" she asked, frowning at him as she turned her face
away. She found the smell of him repulsive. It was as though he
hadn't bathed in days.

"What I'm saying is that I can protect you in ways that he
can't." Conner reached out and brushed a strand of hair out of
Maribel's face, smiling lewdly. "Be with me, Maribel, and you
will no longer have to fear Temper."

Maribel shied away from Conner's touch as if it had burned
her skin. "Stop this, Conner! I don't know what's gotten into you
lately, but Nethaneal has only come to help us. And I'm not sure
what you think you can do that he can't."

"Lot's of things, I assure you," Conner said with a hard,
forced laugh. He wanted more than anything to tell her that he
had gained Temper's favor and was therefore safe from the
dragon's torments, but forced himself to hold his tongue. Now was
not the right time to reveal such an ingenious feat.

"I don't know how many times I've asked you not to bother
me," Maribel said, beginning to feel extreme discomfort. "And I
have no desire to be with you, Conner. I'm sorry to be rude, but
you've left me no other choice but to say it. Now, I'm asking
you Conner, please leave me alone. Please." Maribel shook her
head and made to brush by him, but Conner stepped sideways to

block her path.

"Orion's not here to stop me anymore, is he?" he said, his gaunt face twisting into a menacing sneer as he lowered his face to hers.

Instead of shying away as was her nature to do, Maribel pulled back her hand and slapped Conner hard across the face without even a second thought. "Don't you ever mention Orion's name again, you swine! He died saving my life," she hissed, her green eyes blazing with heated anger. She looked Conner up and down with open disgust. "And just what are you, hmm? You're a skinny, coward...rabbit farmer! You're nothing, and you never will be!"

"You don't know **what** I am!" Conner shot back, his pale face reddening with anger.

"I don't care what you are and what you aren't, Conner. I never have, and I never will! Now get out of my way," Maribel snapped, forcefully shouldering past Conner and striding off down the alleyway with her basket of potatoes swinging at her side.

His rail-thin body trembling with restrained fury, Conner stood watching Maribel as she disappeared down the rows of huts, his dark eyes round with unbelievable **anger**.

How **dare** she speak to him in such a foul way, after all that he had done for her. The foolish girl had no idea who she was talking to, or what she had just done.

No idea.

CHAPTER 22

The sting of Maribel's slap still burning hot on his cheek,
Conner was storming down a side street, his face sharp with
anger.

The Dragon Slayer had turned Maribel against him, Conner
realized with seething hatred. Everything had been going so
beautifully. Conner had spent months patiently courting Maribel,
proving his undying love for her in every way he knew how. And
then Temper had mercifully killed Orion, removing the last
obstacle remaining between their love. It had been fate for them
to marry.

But then that idiot Dragon Slayer had come and turned
Maribel against him.

Conner spat in the dust and cursed nastily as he walked
through the village.

The only reason Maribel seemed to have taken a liking to
Nethaneal at all was--as far as Conner could see--because he'd
come with his strange new weapon claiming the ability to slay
Temper. Like the rest of the villagers, Maribel was deathly
afraid of Temper, and would invest her hope in anyone she
believed could slay the dragon--even if that person was someone
as pompous and arrogant as this Nethaneal Morris.

There was only one solution: Make sure that any plan to kill
Temper ended in utter failure.

Conner had already gone to Tempaer's lair to warn the dragon
of Nethaneal's intentions--a remarkable feat in itself. But what
if that wasn't enough? What if the Dragon Slayer still somehow
succeeded in slaying Temper? Maribel would only become more
infatuated with Nethaneal, that's what, forever ruining Conner's
chances with her.

Conner **could not** let that happen.

Knowing he needed to do more, Conner was contemplating what
else he could do to ensure Nethaneal's failure when suddenly he
noticed the Dragon Slayer's tent standing in the grass at the far
end of the meadow outside the village.

Conner stopped in the middle of the street and narrowed his
eyes, a group of boys playing with a yapping puppy nearby.

Earlier Conner had seen the Dragon Slayer speaking to a man
down at the lake's edge, jotting ridiculous notes into his log.
That was all he seemed to do: Ask questions, scribble nonsense,
and walk around examining the village from all different angles.

The Dragon Slayer would do this all day, day in and day out, and still everyone believed he was capable of slaying Temper. The dolts.

Guessing the Dragon Slayer would stay preoccupied with his notes for the rest of the day, Conner glanced both ways down the dirt street to make sure he wasn't being watched. The group of boys and their puppy had began moving on, leaving only an old man who was busy gingerly emptying his chamber pot into the ditch outside his hut.

Slipping down a narrow side alley, Conner made his way between the rows of huts to the meadow's edge. There he stopped to discretely glance around once more. Seeing no one at this end of the village, Conner ran, stooped at the waist, across the hundred yard stretch of tall grass. Coming to the Dragon Slayer's campsite, Conner jogged around the side of the tent and slipped out of view from the village. Taking a moment to catch his breath, Conner quickly surveyed the area.

A dirt perimeter had been cleared in the grass for a firepit ringed with stones. The pit had gone cold, filled with blackened ash and the charred remnants of a log. Across from the firepit the Dragon Slayer's covered wagon was parked at the edge of the forest. His team of giant black horses were tethered alongside it, all of them having raised their attention up from the grass to stare at him with perked-up ears as they chewed.

Catching his breath, Conner straightened up and checked over his shoulder to make sure he hadn't been followed before ducking through the leather flap of the tent's doorway.

Once inside, Conner found himself in a small, yet neatly-organized space. There was a cot to the left of the doorway, two large wooden trunks across from it, with a desk and squat stool.

Licking his lips as his pulse began to hammer with excitement, Conner rushed over and knelt down beside the trunks. Not quite sure what he was looking for, but knowing that he needed to find something he could use against the Dragon Slayer, Conner unlatched the first trunk's lid and opened it up.

Inside he found nothing but ledgers and stacks of parchment bundled together with twine. Frantically riffling through them, Conner found that the ledgers and parchment contained nothing but scribbled notes and odd drawings of dragons and landscapes.

Conner quickly moved on to the next trunk, finding only neatly folded clothes, a sword, various bottles of strange spices, and a large pouch filled with coins.

Knowing there had to be something in here he could use against the Dragon Slayer, Conner then got down on his hands and knees to check under the cot, finding nothing of use but a pair of boots. He moved on to the desk. There he only found several more sheets of parchment, a compass, an inkwell, and a pile of roasted almond shells from the Dragon Slayer's last snack.

"Damnit!" Conner hissed in frustration, lacing his fingers atop his head as his eyes darted around the tent's interior. It was then that he saw it: A large, iron-banded wooden keg standing in the corner by the doorway.

Dark eyes narrowing with intrigue, Conner dropped his hands
from atop his head and padded across the tent. Kneeling down
beside the barrel, he worked one of his thin fingers under the
wooden lid and pried it open to look inside.

Filling the barrel nearly three-quarters of the way to the
top was what looked like black sand. Curious, Conner reached into
the barrel and scooped up a handful of the strange powder,
wondering what it could be. Then he remembered: It was the
strange powder the Dragon Slayer had used in his demonstration,
when he'd blown the oak tree clear off its trunk.

Conner's top lip curled in a sneer as he raised his bony
fist and watched the stream of granules sift out of his hand like
an hourglass. So **this** was what the Dragon Slayer was planning to
use against Temper, was he?

A nasty grin spread across Conner's gaunt face as the last
of the black powder drained from his fist. If he remembered
correctly, the Dragon Slayer had poured this powder down into
that odd iron tube and touched it with a spark by jerking back on
a lanyard. It must've been this powder which had reacted so
violently, exploding and sending the iron ball smashing clear
through the tree.

Conner tapped his finger against the rim of the barrel as he
sat kneeling on the floor for a time, wondering how exactly he
could sabotage the Dragon Slayer's curious powder.

Obviously, it was a highly flammable substance. If there was

only something he could mix in with it to make it less flammable,
therefore decreasing the force of its reaction and diluting its
power. But Conner would need to do it in such a way as to go
unnoticed by the Dragon Slayer until the time came to face
Temper. It would have to be something dark...something
unflammable...

The answer, a pure stroke of genius, came to Conner only a
moment later: The black ash, from the firepit just outside the
tent.

Scrambling to his feet, Conner ducked out of the tent and
hurried out to the cold firepit. There he shoved the charred log
aside and scooped both hands down into the pit, gathering up as
much of the ash and blackened earth as he could hold. Carrying it
like a priceless substance in both hands, Conner then stood up,
shouldered through the tent's doorflap, and made his way over to
the keg in the corner. Being careful not to spill any, he dumped
the ash on top of the powder, picked out several pebbles, then
stirred it together. Three more times he made this trip from the
firepit back to the barrel, each time mixing in more earth and
ash until adding anymore would have raised the level of powder in
the keg to an obvious level.

Arms blackened up to the elbows, Conner hurriedly wiped his
hands clean on his shirt before fitting the lid back on the keg
just as he'd found it so as not to catch the Dragon Slayer's
attention. Once done, Conner strode to the doorway of the tent,
pausing to smile with malicious excitement at the Dragon

Slayer's space.

Let's see you be the hero **now**, he thought, his small dark
eyes gleaming hatefully.

Then Conner slipped out of the tent and was gone.

CHAPTER 23

Late that night Nethaneal sat at his desk by the soft glow
of candlelight. Unable to sleep, he wore a white shirt tied
loosely across his muscular chest, his golden hair tied back out
of his face as he studied the many sheets of parchment fanned out
before him.

Before attempting to slay any dragon, Nethaneal always made
it a point to collect every scrap of information he could find
about it. When dealing with such fearsome, violent beasts, one
could never know too much concerning their individual habits,
their tendencies, their strengths, or especially their
weaknesses. Once in possession of this knowledge, Nethaneal could
then formulate a strategy around what he'd learned to help slay
the dragon.

But thus far, all of his research into Temper had only led
Nethaneal to more and more questions: What kind of dragon has

such heat as to melt iron? Is so large that it can swallow cattle
whole, yet seems to prefer feasting on humans? Is so ferocious
that it attacks a village in the middle of the day, and is so
arrogant it takes a king's castle as its lair?

   None of it made sense. Before traveling to this village,
he'd never encountered a dragon like Temper.

   Nethaneal set his quill down to rub his forehead, the golden
candlelight shimmering in his blue eyes as he continued to review
his notes.

   He would have to find a way to lure Temper away from his
castle, since trying to ambush the dragon in its own lair would
be akin to walking into a death trap. Also, by all reports the
dragon's attacks on the village were infrequent and violently
sudden, so waiting for Temper to return was highly impractical.
Then there was the question of how Nethaneal would actually kill
the dragon once brought face to face with the beast. He knew that
a single cannon shot, no matter how accurate the blow, would be
insufficient to topple a dragon of such size and nasty
temperment. And if all of these questions were not precisely
answered and braided into one flawless course of action,
Nethaneal knew he would be killed and the villagers forced to pay
the price for Temper's wrath. He could not let them down, not
after all that they'd been through.

   Further compounding these problems was the issue of Conner,
the scrawny, dark-haired rabbit farmer that Nethaneal had seen
disappearing into Temper's castle. Surely a dragon as vicious as

Temper would not allow anyone to waltz freely into his lair and then depart with their lives without getting something very valuable in return. So **what** had Conner been doing there? And why?

Whatever the answer to this question happened to be, Nethaneal knew it didn't bode well for him, nor his intentions to slay the dragon. Numerous times over the past ten days Nethaneal had been out in the village collecting information when he'd happened to glance up from his notes just in time to see Conner-- his gaunt, pale face, framed by his oily black hair--sneering hatefully at him from a distance. And then he'd be gone, every time leaving Nethaneal with an unsettling feeling deep in his gut. Being a seasoned Dragon Slayer, Nethaneal had learned to trust this instinct which only meant one thing: Danger.

Conner, Nethaneal knew, was in cohorts with the dragon.

Nethaneal had considered confronting Conner with this, but had quickly thought better of it. At the right time, and at the right place, Nethaneal could surely use this information to his benefit. Until that time came, however, he would have to keep it a secret from everyone that Conner was a traitor--especially from Conner himself. If he found out that he'd been exposed, the sneaky double-crosser might feel compelled to try something brash.

A blizzard of thoughts swirling in his mind, Nethaneal paused to rub his sore eyes. It was then that he heard his horses tethered outside the tent nicker and snort in agitation, followed by muffled footsteps brushing through the tall grass.

Pulled from his rumination, Nethaneal stood up, producing with one deft movement a sharp, gleaming dagger from his waistband which he held low near his thigh.

"Who's there?" he called through the tent's doorflap, suspicious it was Conner sneaking up to his tent. Anyone crazy enough to waltz into a dragon's lair was not someone it was wise to underestimate.

Outside the footsteps stopped. Then, quite timidly, a woman's hushed voice said, "Nethaneal...it's me, Maribel."

Releasing a sigh of exasperation for allowing his thoughts to run amuck and cause him to overreact, Nethaneal tucked his dagger back into his waistband and said, "Yes, Maribel. Please, come in." He had spoken with her earlier in the day near the butcher's shop, and hadn't been expecting her so late. He was surprised at how happy he felt to again have her company.

Pushing through the doorflap, Maribel emerged from the darkness outside and into the soft, golden aura of candlelight filling the tent. She wore a plain white dress which accentuated her curvaceous figure, her long brown hair falling to her shoulders in gentle curls and framing her open, pretty face. She was smiling beautifully and holding in her upturned palms a dish covered with a brown cloth.

"Maribel," Nethaneal said, taking in the sight of her, "To what do I owe the honor?"

Maribel smiled shyly at his compliment and offered the dish out to him. "Nothing but lamb pie, I assure you. I got some meat

from the butcher after we spoke earlier, and had some left over.
I hope you're hungry."

Nethaneal smiled, pleasantly surprised by the gift. "I'm
starved. How did you know? Oh, it smells wonderful. Thank you,
Maribel. You shouldn't have."

As Nethaneal took the pie and found a place to set it,
Maribel tucked a strand of hair behind her ear and curiously
glanced around the tent's neatly arranged interior, noticing the
many sheets of parchment spread across his desk.

"I hope I wasn't interrupting anything...?" she asked,
worried she'd come at a bad time. She would have come earlier,
but she'd worked for hours on that pie, getting it just right.

Setting the pie down, Nethaneal straightened up and batted a
hand at the desk. "Not at all. I needed a break anyway. I've been
giving myself a headache all evening."

"I don't mean to be intrusive," Maribel said, frowning, "But
what is it you're always writing on those papers you carry around
with you?"

"Information. Notes. Ideas. But as of lately, it seems to be
mostly questions I haven't been able to answer," Nethaneal said.
Seeing the concerned puzzlement in Maribel's eyes, he smiled and
politely lifted his hand in a gesture for her to have a seat.
"Please, allow me to explain."

"...Alright," Maribel said, smoothing the back of her dress
as she sat on the edge of his cot.

Taking a seat on the wooden stool beside his desk, Nethaneal

gathered up the stack of parchment he'd been reviewing and tapped
them into order. "What I've written here are all accounts
describing Temper from people I've spoken with. You see, before I
attempt to slay your dragon, I must know everything there is to
know about him. His personality. His disposition. His strengths.
His weaknesses."

"Aren't all dragons the same? Awfull, like Temper?" Maribel
wondered. She couldn't imagine them being any other way.

"Certainly not. Some of them are similar in appearance, but
just like you or I, no two dragons are exactly alike."

"How so?" Maribel asked, turning her head curiously.

Nethaneal chewed the corner of his lip as he thought of a
way to explain it to her. "Think about some of the people that
you know, specifically their personalities," he began. "You will
see that each has their own characteristics. One might be kind,
while another's a thief. Some are brave, and others are cowardly.
The same goes for dragons, really. A portion of this is
determined by their breed, but certainly not all."

"Breeds? You mean there's different...**kinds** of dragons?"
Maribel asked, a note of alarm in her words.

"Oh, there's many, depending on the area," Nethaneal said,
as offhandedly as if he were discussing different types of ducks
instead of fire breathing, flesh eating beasts. Before Maribel
could inquire further, Nethaneal stood and walked across the tent
to an iron-banded trunk. There he opened the lid, reached down
inside, and retrieved a large, leather-bound book which he handed

to Maribel as he came back. "This is a log containing all the different types of dragons I've encountered in my travels. Have a look."

Taking the heavy book and setting it across her knees, Maribel folded open the leather-bound cover, her green eyes widening in astonishment. On the page before her was a masterfully hand-drawn picture of a dragon unlike Maribel could have ever imagined.

Drawn bearing its teeth as it emerged from the shadowy depths of a rocky cave, the dragon's head was incredibly wide and flat, like a shovel, lacking horns but still utterly terrifying. Instead of a long sweeping neck like Temper's, this dragon's head barely left its hunched, scaly shoulders. Its body was compact and powerful, bristling with thick armored plates. Wings which looked too small for its body were tucked at its sides. Its short legs held it crouched low to the ground, its stubby tail ending at a mace-like ball of spikes.

Nethaneal leaned forward on his stool to see which picture she was looking at, and said, "That's a Subterranean Rock Jaw. Tough basterds, although they can't fly very well. They live underground, mostly, hidden away in caves or dens. They tend to be elusive, and very hard to find. Mostly it's farmers who pay me to kill them for eating their livestock. Rock Jaws aren't much of a threat to humans unless one happens to stumble across its lair."

Curious as to what other kinds of dragons there were,

Maribel turned the page to the next drawing.

In this one, a dragon stood poised in an almost dignified stance amongst a lush forest of tall pine trees, head held high. The dragon had two mighty horns which swept up off its brow, and two more jutting out from beneath its chin. Its neck was long and graceful, its scales adorned with an elegant diamond pattern which followed the ridge of its spine all the way to the tip of its tail.

"That's a Western Noble Hornbeard," Nethaneal explained. "They live in forests and along mountain ranges. A very intelligent breed. I tracked one for weeks once, only to discover that it had purposely led me to a bear's den instead of its lair. It was an unpleasant ordeal, to say the least."

Both amused by Nethaneal's story and impressed by his knowledge of dragons, Maribel smiled as she slid her finger along the parchment's edge and again turned the page.

"Oh...," she cringed at the drawing before her, her smile vanishing,""It's so ugly."

It was Nethaneal's turn to smile as he watched her reaction to the drawings. "Indeed. That's a Saw-Toothed Mud Slinger. Nasty beasts. They live in swamps."

The drawing showed a leprous-looking dragon in the process of erupting out of the stagnant waters of a swamp. Needle-like spines with membranous webs of flesh stretched between them were flared menacingly from both sides of its elongated head. Its snarling mouth was filled with jagged, irregular teeth. Scraps of slime clung to its scales, and webs of flesh were stretched between its hooked claws.

"They submerge themselves in swamp water so that they can't be seen, leaving only their eyes and nostrils above the surface, then ambush anything that travels past," Nethaneal explained.

"Then how do you find them?" Maribel asked.

"Simple, really: Their smell. It's horribly pungent, even while they're under water. I can't describe it with any measure of justice, but once you smell it, you're already too close. It's enough to make a grown man gag."

Almost reluctant to touch it, Maribel turned the page over. This time, her reaction to what she saw was quite the opposite. "My--it's beautiful!" she exclaimed, covering her mouth as her eyes widened in amazement.

This drawing showed a large dragon soaring through the air above an endless expanse of rolling ocean waters. Its wings were magnificently patterned, fanned out at its sides with all four legs tucked back in flight. Two horns jutted straight forward from its brow, long neck arched as it seemed to search the rolling waters below. Just like its wings, the dragon's scaled flanks were finely adorned with jeweled patterns which flowed gracefully down the length of its body to the tip of its hooked tail.

"What kind of dragon is this?" Maribel asked, glancing up at Nethaneal in amazement.

Nethaneal's handsome face glowed in the candlelight. He was

enjoying this time alone with Maribel, he realized, even if it
was while doing something as mundane as discussing dragons.

"It's a Barbed-Tailed Pirater," he said. "They dwell along
ocean cliffs. Their entire bodies, even their wings and eyes, are
the same shade of blue as the sky, which makes them very
difficult to see while out on the open water until they're right
upon you. They prey mostly on whales and sealions, but
occasionally they'll attack ships. It's a growing problem with
trading vessels."

"That's amazing," Maribel said, fixated on the drawing.
After a moment she looked up and asked, "How did you get into
this? Slaying dragons, I mean?"

The pleasant look on Nethaneal's face slowly faded. His
eyes fell away from hers as he cleared his throat, visibly
discomforted by her question.

"It wasn't by choice, I assure you," he began with a weak
attempt at a smile. "I grew up in a family of simple woodsmen. My
mother, father, two brothers and I lived off the land, trapping
fur in the Akashian mountains. One morning my father asked me to
go down to the stream and fill a pail of water for breakfast, so
I went. I was just a boy--seven years old, about. When I got to
the stream and started filling the pail, I heard a terrifying
noise, a roar, echoing off the mountains, from the direction of
our home. It was like noghing I had ever heard. I was frightened,
so I ran back to see what had happened."

Nethaneal sighed, his blue eyes distant as he recalled the

memory. "There was a dragon--it looked as big as a mountain to me--snapping at the milk cow tethered outside our home. I was watching from the trees. I couldn't move. I couldn't breathe. I had never seen such a frightening creature in all my life."

Maribel listened intently to Nethaneal's story, watching as the pain of the distant memory etched itself across his face.

"My father and two older brothers came running out of the house, yelling and shooting arrows at the dragon, trying to scare it off before it ate our cow. It turned on them instead. My father and brothers were brave and tried to fight, but they stood no chance. It ate all three of them. My mother came out of the house screaming, and the dragon roared flame over her and our home before flying away."

Nethaneal shook his head with regret, his jaw muscles flexing as he clenched his teeth. "I didn't know what to do. I was too frightened to move. So I just stood there, trembling, watching helplessly as my family was killed and my home was burned to ashes...I should have done something."

A knot had formed inside Maribel's throat. She opened her mouth to speak, but couldn't find the words to express her sympathy, so she reached out and put a comforting hand on his knee. She knew all too well the pain he had gone through.

Nethaneal put his hand over hers before going on. "The next thing I remember is running as fast as I could. Rocks, bushes, trees, all rushing past me. I was alone for two days in the mountains before I found my way back to the city. But once I got

there I couldn't find anyone to help me. Thought I was a lying
little begger making up wild stories, I suppose. I was hungry and
desperate, so I volunteered to work for food at the nearest port
as a deckhand."

He paused as he reflected back on the memory. "It was a
rough life, especially for a boy as young as I was. I swabbed
decks, cooked, emptied the chamberpots--anything the sailors
themselves wouldn't do. Often they would get drunk and beat me
for the fun of it. Sometimes we'd spend months at sea without
ever seeing land, sailing from port to port trading goods. With
so much time on my hands, I taught myself how to read and write.
And to draw, of course. That was my favorite thing to do while I
had time to myself, looking out over all that blue water, drawing
things I'd seen.

"For ten years I sailed the oceans like this, growing into a
man on the deck of a ship. It was amazing at times, seeing
different lands, different people, different cultures. But still
I felt empty. I suppose the guilt of not trying to stop that
dragon from killing my family, of having not done anything at
all, sapped any enjoyment I could have had in life.

"Then, around my eighteenth birthday, our ship sailed into a
trading port on the Chinese coast. It was there that I first
learned of black powder, a powerful substance the Chinese people
had created. Sailors couldn't get enough of it. They were using
the explosive powder in cannons to sink pirate ships on the open
seas. It was the newest, most powerful weapon anyone had ever

seen.

"I, however, had a different idea: If these weapons,
cannons, were powerful enough to rip entire ships apart, then why
not use them to kill dragons instead? I saw it as my second
chance for having not done anything to save my own family. So I
took all my savings and bought my own cannon and keg of powder,
and haven't looked back since."

Nethaneal gently squeezed Maribel's hand as he came out of
the memory, glancing over at her with his deep blue eyes. "That's
why I've come here, Maribel. I know how it feels to lose
everything to a dragon. I don't wish that kind of pain on
anyone. I'll do anything I can to prevent others from suffering
the way I did."

"I'm so sorry," Maribel said, her voice a whisper. Feeling
the sting of tears brought to her eyes by Nethaneal's
heartbreaking story, she shook her head and sniffed, taking a
moment to compose herself. She then retracted her hand from
beneath Nethaneal's and again turned her attention to the large
book spread across her lap.

"What breed is Temper?" she asked, wanting to change the
subject. "I haven't seen his kind in here."

"Mmm," Nethaneal gave a thoughtful grimace, "That's what's
been troubling me."

Nethaneal stood up and turned, sitting down on the cot
beside Maribel. He was so close to her that Maribel could smell
the scent of him: A musk of exotic spices and wood smoke, so

alluring that Maribel found herself savoring the draft of air which had followed him. She caught herself; though, and forced her attention back onto what Nethaneal was showing her.

"Your dragon, Temper, is unlike any dragon that I have ever encountered," Nethaneal said, reaching over and flipping through pages showing various breeds of dragons he'd slain. "He could be an all together new breed which has yet to be discovered. But, considering his size and disposition, I find this doubtful. People would remember dragons like this."

"What is he, then?" Maribel asked, studying the side of Nethaneal's cleanly shaved face by the glow of candlelight.

Nethaneal flipped through several more pages before stopping on one in particular. This picture showed an awe-inspiring scene of a gargantuan dragon perched at the top of a craggy mountain peak, horned head raised high on an arched neck, massive wings spread so wide they blocked out the sun, its rays exploding out from behind the god-like dragon.

"That's him!" Maribel insisted, tapping the picture with her finger. "That's Temper--his breed, I mean."

"By the looks of it, yes," Nethaneal conceded, touching the knuckle of a curled finger to his chin in deep, troubled thought. "This breed of dragon is known as a Night-Bringing Colossus. They can grow so large that they block out the sun when they take to the sky, casting all below them into darkness."

Maribel supressed a shudder, remembering all too well the icy horror which had shocked her body as Temper's shadow fell over their village. If it hadn't been for Orion, she and her father never would have lived past that awful morning.

"But this looks just like Temper," Maribel said, sadly shaking off the memory of her twin brother and the tears it threatened to bring if she dwelled on it a second longer.

"If Temper does belong to this particular breed, then he's an unusual one," Nethaneal observed. "Night-Bringing Colossuses such as these are exceedingly rare, covering large tracks of land. Not only that, their temperments are known to be very docile--for a dragon, anyway--only hunting when they need to feed, and only then on much larger creatures, such as bears and cattle and horses. Very seldom will a Colossus prey on a human. We're simply too snall a meal for all the trouble."

"Temper's evil, is all," Maribel said, hate lacing her words. "He likes to kill."

Nethaneal shrugged. "I don't doubt it at all. But that doesn't explain everything. Temper's bite is venomous, you see. Colussuse's are not. In fact, no other breed of dragon in the world is known to be venomous. Except for one."

"Which is it?" Maribel asked, ingrigued.

Reaching over, Nethaneal flipped a page in the book and tapped his finger on the page. "This one. The Plague-Tongued Death Reaper."

Staring at the picture, Maribel felt the blood drain from her face as goose flesh prickled down her arms. It was horrible.

What stared out from the surface of the parchment was what

looked like a demonic entity which had assumed the form of a
dragon. Its head was diamond-shaped and flat, like that of a
viper's, with slitted eyes and three barbed horns flaring out
from each side of its snarling face. Its scales were as black as
obsidian, a bristling row of deadly sharp spines traveling down
the ridge of its back to the barbed end of its tail. Its teeth
were as long and sharp as icicles, a black forked tongue
slighering snake-like out from between them.

     "They're a much smaller breed of dragon, but by far the
deadliest. They're also nocturnal, meaning they hunt by the
cover of darkness." Nethaneal frowned slightly at the drawing as
he sat on the cot beside Maribel, as if even he were unsettled by
what he saw. "It's odd. Most dragons attack humans only out of
hunger or fear--there's no malice involved. But Death Reapers are
a peculiar sort. They seem to actually **enjoy** hunting humans,
causing fear and pain. No one knows exactly why. Just vicious by
nature, I assume."

     "Have you ever killed one of these?" Maribel asked, turning
her face towards Nethaneal but continuing to stare at the awful
picture as if unable to look away.

     "One," Nethaneal answered grimly. "And I was fortunate to
have survived. Luckily, they're the rarest of all breeds. It's
believed they're simply too vicious to reproduce in any great
numbers."

     "So what does this dragon have to do with Temper?" Maribel
asked.

"Quite a lot, I'm afraid." Nethaneal looked away, thoughts
churning behind his eyes in the wavering candlelight. "After all
the information I've gathered on Temper, I've become convinced
that he is a hybrid--the product of a union between a Colossus
and a Death Reaper. I can't imagine how it happened, but I'm sure
it did. Temper, the huge, nasty, venomous beast that he is, is
the result."

Maribel frowned as she looked down at the awful picture
opened in her lap. "But Temper looks nothing like this," she
worried, "How can that be?"

"Simple. Think about when a couple has a child. Sometimes it
will take after its mother, other times its father. Obviously,
Temper was born with the outward appearance of a Colossus, but
with the venom and nasty disposition of a Death Reaper. The worst
possible combination I can imagine." Nethaneal rubbed his chin.
"I have never seen the likes of a dragon such as this," he
admitted.

Not wanting to see any more dragons, Maribel snapped the boo
book closed and set it aside. "But you can kill him, can't you?"
she asked worriedly.

Emerging from his thoughts, Nethaneal answered with some
reluctance, "I can. But I assure you that it will not be easy.
Underestimating a dragon such as Temper is a death wish."

"How will you do it?"

"I have a plan, but I can't reveal it until the time's
right." Nethaneal smiled slyly. "You'll understand why soon

enough."

Maribel hesitated, then looked at the Dragon Slayer with a
sad sort of sincerity. "No one here really thinks you can do it--
kill Temper, I mean. They've all lost hope. But...I know that you
can. I believe in you, Nethaneal, even if others don't."

It was then that Nethaneal and Maribel locked eyes, and for
a spontaneous, suspended moment everything--even the grief of
loss and the fear of the upcoming battle with Temper--dissolved
into mist around them. Suddenly it was only the two of them,
sitting close inside a tent, Nethaneal's blue eyes piercing deep
into the beautiful green of Maribel's, their bodies only inches
from one another's.

"I wouldn't dare let you down, Maribel," Nethaneal said as
he continued to stare into her enchanting, jade-green eyes.
Unable to restrain himself, he reached up and caressed the smooth
surface of her cheek, gently turning her face up to his. "Not
ever."

Maribel leaned into the warmth of Nethaneal's strong, gentle
touch, again becoming intensely aware of the spicy musk of his
skin, of the way the muscles in his chest and arms bulged against
the fabric of his shirt...

Quite abruptly Maribel realized what she was doing and shot
to her feet, dropping her gaze to the floor in embarrassment.
"Yes, well," she stammered, smoothing the front of her dress with
trembling hands. "I trust you will not let us down, Nethaneal. I
must go, it's getting late. I--I hope you enjoy the pie."

"I will, Maribel. And thank you again--" Nethaneal said, getting to his feet to see her out.

But Maribel had already hurried out of the tent, the leather doorflap swaying in the darkness.

CHAPTER 24

Urick stood in the shimmering hot air over the bed of coals
in his smithy, sweat dripping off his grimy, determined face as
he hammered a glowing length of iron.

Ever since Temper's last devastating attack on the village,
Urick had been hard at work over the coals every day from sunup
to sundown. There were numerous wheel studs and axel caps to mend
for ruined carts and wagons; new bands to be hammered flat for
kegs which had been shattered; tools to be forged, harnesses to
be fashioned, horseshoes to make, as well as a long list of
various other orders to fill. And because of the Dragon Slayer's
expensive bounty, most of the villagers could only afford to pay
Urick pennies for his labor. It was almost too much for one man
to take on without becoming overwhelmed.

Using tongs to push the length of iron back into the coals

to soften the metal, Urick mopped his brow with a rag and turned
with his hand extended. "Orion, hand me the bellows..."

The words had barely left Urick's mouth when he felt the
painful blow to his heart, the sickening drop of his stomach.

The small shop, its work tables cluttered with waiting
projects and tools, was entirely empty.

From the time he could walk Orion had kept Urick company in
this very shop. As a toddler he'd padded around after Urick,
asking what this was, what that was, crying whenever he banged or
burned his curious little fingers, but mostly staring up at Urick
as he worked with those big green eyes full of wonder and
astonishment.

Through much trial and error, sweat and tears, Orion had
grown up here. And in doing so, he had not only learned to mold
iron to his will, but also the values of hard work, honesty, and
discipline which make up a man. There had been arguments. There
had been laughter. But always there had been the deep
companionship that exists only between a father and a son, a bond
so deep it is unlike any other.

Surveying the empty workshop with his pained green eyes,
Urick realized for the first time that Orion was truly gone. All
the memories, all the hopes for his son's future, all the
dreams...Gone in an instant, vanished down the gullet of a
monster to satisfy its sick, temporary hunger. The same hunger
which had stolen his beloved wife, Charlotte, all those years
before, leaving Urick with a broken heart and two small children

to raise on his own.

Miserable tears welling in his eyes, Urick took in a hitching breath and leaned his calloused hands on the workbench, dropped his head between his thick shoulders, and began to cry. Not a man who succomed easily to emotions, Urick's tears at first came in slow, restrained sobs. But the pain and the loss was simply too great, even for a man as strong as him to bear, and it forced its way to the surface in a groundswell of sorrow as powerful as an eruption.

Urick cried out loud as he leaned his weight on the workbench, suddenly too weak to stand, his fists clenched in his sweat-dampened hair. Tears flowed from his eyes, his heart feeling as though it were a thing of fabric being slowly ripped down the middle. Temper had taken so much away from him that Urick felt as though the monstrous dragon had actually reached into his chest and ripped out a chunk of his soul, wounds which would never heal. His beloved wife Charlotte, his dear son Orion...Gone, forever....

It wasn't fair. It should have been him. It **should have been him**.

Urick was still crying, his fists clutched in his hair as he stood with his elbows leaned on the cluttered workbench, when Maribel ducked into the shop from the daylight outside, a basket in her hands.

"Good morning, father," she said, not noticing her father's state as she made her way to a workbench and began clearing an area to set the basket. "I brought you something to eat. You left before I could make you a proper breakfast, so this will have to do. Promise me you'll eat all of it. You've been working far too much not to--"

It was there that Maribel cut herself off, realizing that something was wrong. Frowning at her father, who stood across the shop doubled over a workbench, Maribel asked, "...Father, are you alright?"

Urick lifted his head from between his shoulders, his back still turned to his daughter as he leaned over the workbench. "I miss them," was all he said. He shook his head and again lowered it between his shoulders, his broad back hitching.

Hearing the tears in her father's words, Maribel emitted a light gasp and covered her mouth. Finding her father doubled over crying in the middle of his workshop stopped her dead in her tracks. Although he was a gentle man, her father had always possessed the silent, unbending strength of the iron he forged. She had never once seen him cry when her mother or brother were killed, never even heard him complain when red-hot metal scorched away his skin.

Dropping her hands as tears welled and spilled from her own eyes, Maribel said, "Oh, father!" and hurried across the workshop to him.

His grimy, weathered face twisted with pain, Urick stood and took his daughter in his arms, hugging her tightly against him as the two stood crying together in their awful, shared anguish.

"I love you, Maribel. I want you to know that," Urick said,
holding his daughter close. She was his pride, his joy, his last
reason to go on living in this cruel, brutal world. "I love you
so much...You're all that I have left."

CHAPTER 25


"I think 'es a turd, meself."

"I haven't liked the looks o' him since he got here."

"Me neither."

"Loogit 'im, lousy slapstick. Does nothin' all day but scribble in a ledger. What kinda man needs to know a thing about readin' and writin' anyhow?"

The four men stood in a group at the bar, drinking ale as they scowled across the smoky pub at the Dragon Slayer. There, Nethaneal sat alone at a table in the corner, his back turned, casually sipping a mug of ale while busy writing in his log.

"Too pretty, yeh ask me. How's he 'posed to kill Temper if all he does is prance around the village, flusterin' up all the women?" one man with a greasy face said.

"Las' week, caught my wife starin' at him in the market."

Hadta knock a bit o' sense into her, I did," said another short, powerful-looking man standing amongst the group.

Right then Horris lumbered over with two mugs in each one of his huge hands and set them on the bar for the group of men. Noticing their rigid stances and scowling faces, he frowned as he wiped his hands and asked, "There a problem here, gents?"

The tallest man in the group grunted with disgust before picking up his mug and motioning across the pub with his elbow. "Our problem's sittin' right over there. Dragon Slayer... Bollocks. He's a fraud, you ask me. Hasn't done nothin' but get all the women cluckin' like hens. I say we wallop the pretty right outta him. See how tough he is then."

Grumbling their agreements, the three other men all picked up their mugs and continued to scowl at the Dragon Slayer as they drank.

Horris followed their gazes across the smoky pub to where Nethaneal sat and grunted humorlessly. He had never made it a secret that he didn't like this man Nethaneal Morris. Even with his fancy weapon Horris doubted he could slay Temper, and here he was getting everyone's hopes up. It wasn't that Horris didn't want to see that basterd dragon dead—he did, just as much as anyone else in this village—he just didn't want anymore hurt and disappointment to come to his friends and family. And this was exactly what he feared would happen if too much trust was invested in the cocky, self-assured Dragon Slayer who so far had done nothing but scribble notes in a log.

Personally, Horris thought Nethaneal could benefit from a
bit of physical humbling.

"Well, what's stoppin' you boys?" Horris asked the group of
men. Out of respect for Urick, **he** couldn't give the fraud a good
thrashing, but he could certainly turn a blind eye while a group
of drunken patrons did.

Knowing that Horris never allowed fighting in his pub, the
group of men turned and looked questioningly at him. When Horris
merely shrugged his broad shoulders indifferently, the four men
laughed and quickly guzzled down the last of their ale. Then,
slamming down their empty mugs and wiping their mouths, they
started across the pub, shoving tables and chairs out of their
way.

Nethaneal was reviewing his thick stack of notes concerning
Temper, busy putting the final touches on his plan, when suddenly
he noticed that the pub had gone silent around him, all the
drunkenly idle chatter and thick laughter having ended quite
abruptly. Then he felt a smart tap on his left shoulder followed
by a rough voice which said, "Hey, **Dragon Slayer**...what say we
have a quick word, eh?"

Although only one of them had spoke, Nethaneal could sense
the presence of the other men standing close behind him, could
feel the patrons' eyes watching in the anticipating silence.

Something very bad was about to happen.

Surprisingly, Nethaneal managed a pleasant smile as he very
deliberately laid down his feather quill, shut his log, slid back

his chair, and stood up from the table. Turning around, he saw four troublesome-looking men gathered in a half-circle before him, all scowling and cracking their knuckles. The other patrons had collectively left their tables and backed out of the way, waiting in bated silence for the violence to begin.

Behind the bar, Horris smirked as he wiped out a mug. He of all people wanted to see this.

"What seems to be the occasion, gentlemen?" Nethaneal asked, eyes tracking aaross the four mens' faces.

"The õ-casion is that we don't like you here no more," the shortest man in the group said, jutting his chin forward.

"Yeah. Seems to us, we agreed to pay you to kill Temper, not sit around all day scribblin' nonsense and hobnobbin' with our women," the next man said.

"Gentlemen, let me assure you that slaying a dragon such as Temper is no simple feat. You can't rush into it. A detailed plan must first be--" Nethaneal attempted to explain.

"Shut it!" the biggest man spat. "We'll deal with you in our own way. Won't we, John?"

"Sure will," the greasy-faced man agreed, smiling putridly to reveal blackened stubs of teeth.

As if on cue, one man on each side of the gooup broke off and began stalking around behind Nethaneal, tearing tables and chairs out of their way until the four men surrounded him in a cleared corner of the pub.

"Well...," Nethaneal said with an almost amused smile on his face, "There's no other way out of this, I suppose?"

"'Fraid not," the biggest man said with a blood-hungry grin.

"Very well." Those two simple, calmly spoken words were all
that Nethaneal said before the kindness on his face vanished.
Then his arms lashed out with the speed of two cracking whips,
his splayed fingers jabbing into the eyes of the two men standing
before him. Both men clutched their faces in their hands as they
stumbled backwards, cursing in pain.

With the same whip-crack speed Nethaneal threw his arms
back, elbowing the two men standing behind him hard in the face.
One of them went down cursing, blood gushing from his broken
nose. The other staggered backwards, regained his balance, and
touched his bleeding mouth. When a tooth--looking like a bloody
little corn kernel--fell into his palm, the man threw it aside
and bellowed, "Yer dead!" before lowering his head and charging
across the pub.

"That's it!" Nethaneal challenged, his legs bent readily as
the man rushed him, "Come on!"

At the last second Nethaneal leapt forward and kneed the man
square on the top of the head, knocking him back onto the seat of
his trousers. He dazedly tried to get to his feet, tough with
mean strength, but Nethaneal's boot smashing into the underside
of his jaw sent him sprawling across the dirt floor with his arms
splayed, unconscious.

The largest man in the group rubbed his eyes, blinked back
his vision, and snarled, "You dirty fightin' son of a bitch!" He

rushed at Nethaneal, his balled fist cocked back, and threw a
powerful right punch.

Nethaneal ducked the blow, the man's fist wafting by just
inches over his head. He threw a hard right jab which pushed deep
into the man's soft gut before leaping to the side and sending a
rapid-fire succession of punches hammering against his face. The
large man staggered backwards, head bouncing this way and that
under the pounding assault of fists, before losing his balance an
and crashing through a table.

The patrons, amazed that the handsome young Dragon Slayer
could hold his own even in a group of four scrappy drunks, began
to rally together in their support of him, cheering and whistling
him on. Perhaps that was why a fat woman with a mole on her cheek
pointed and screamed to warn him, "Look out--'es got a knife!"

Nethaneal turned and saw that the shortest man in the group-
a stumpy little block of a man with a bald, round head--was
creeping up behind him with a dagger held low and dangerous in
one hand.

"Who do you think ya're?" he hissed, blood leaking from his
shattered nose spraying on his words. "Come here thinkin' yer so
great. Yer a fraud!"

"I am no fraud," Nethaneal said, loud enough for the entire
pub to hear as he backed away one slow step at a time, knees bent
readily. "And I have come only to kill your dragon. There's no
cause for anyone else to be harmed."

The short, powerful man grinned viciously through his own

mash of dripping blood, his round eyes narrowing with malice. "No--Only you!" he roared, lunging forward and thrusting the dagger at Nethaneal's chest.

Nethaneal caught the man's thick forearm, stopping the dagger in mid-air. With his other arm Nethaneal drove the palm of his hand hard against the short man's blood-slickened face, slipping two fingers up his nostrils and pushing them deep into his broken nose.

"EEAAUUUGH!" the short man raged, his yell a nasally, muffled scream of pain as his head was pushed back.

"Give me the knife," Nethaneal warned, holding the man's forearm with one hand while the fingers of the other were buried in his nose, "Give me the knife, and I'll let you go."

His face swollen as red as an apple, blood smeared across his grimacing teeth, and his eyes wild with rage, the short man didn't seem to want to give up the fight just yet. But when Nethaneal pushed his fingers deeper into his nostrils, grinding the splintered shards of cartilage and bone together, he wailed, "Fine! **FINE!** Take the bloody thing!" and shook the dagger in his fist.

Carefully, Nethaneal slid his hand down the man's forearm, clutched the knife, and relieved it from his grasp. "Thank you," Nethaneal said, pulling his fingers out of the man's nose with two wet pops and stepping back. "This didn't need to happen."

"Piss off, Maggot!" the short man snapped, cupping his bleeding nose as he turned and stormed out of the pub, angrily kicking a chair out of his way.

Three groaning men left sprawled on the dirt floor all around him, Nethaneal wiped the blood off his fingers, gathered up his quill, tucked his log under his arm, and walked to the bar under the amazed stares of the patrons standing silently around the pub. There Nethaneal stabbed the dagger into the bartop in front of Horris so that it stood on end.

"Give this back to him when he calms down, would you?" he asked, nodding to the doorway through which the short, furious man had just departed.

Appearing grudgingly amused, Horris pulled the dagger out of the bartop and tapped it thoughtfully in his palm as he sized up the Dragon Slayer. "Where'd you learn to fight like that?" he asked. The only man Horris had ever known capable of besting four men at once was himself. And even then he didn't walk away unscathed as the Dragon Slayer had just done.

"I grew up on a shipfull of sailors," was the only explanation Nethaneal offered as he casually dug several coins out of his pocket, "How much do I owe you for the ale? Oh, and the table as well."

Reluctant to take a liking to the Dragon Slayer, yet unable to not respect him for his toughness, Horris grunted and returned to wiping out mugs. "It's on the house," he said grudgingly.

Nethaneal smiled, realizing he'd just passed some kind of test by the big man. He tossed up the coins and caught them again with a jangle before returning them to his pocket. "Rather generous of you Horris. You have a good day."

And with that, the Dragon Slayer turned and walked out of the pub under the silent, watchful gaze of the awe-struck patrons.

Once Nethaneal was gone Horris glanced back to the three men, who were all moaning and clutching their wounds as they struggled to get to their feet. Looking disgusted, Horris threw his rag down on the bar and yelled, "Common, yeh damned ninnies, get up! Yer embarrassin' yerselves!"

CHAPTER 26

The following afternoon was overcast with broken tufts of clouds, the slight breeze blowing in off the lake cool but not cold. In the newly rebuilt market merchants were busy hanging their wares on display, calling out to the passersby and shrewdly haggling deals. Women gossiped in scattered groups as they carefully picked over the goods, their children playing and running about in the dusty street where chickens clucked and mangy dogs barked at the men hauling cartloads of hay, feed, wood, and livestock throughout the village. Gray tendrils of wood smoke flowed on the breeze, as did the earthy smell of horse dung and the enticing scent of cooking meat. It was a day like any other in the small lakeside village, blessedly busy and uneventful.

That is, until the Dragon Slayer's massive team of black

horses suddenly came thundering into the marketplace.

Alarmed, the villagers hurriedly cleared out of the street
to avoid the wagon, men pushing carts aside and women corralling
their children to safety as the team of horses came to a halt,
stamping and snorting, a cloud of dust swirling around them.

Sitting atop the covered wagon, Nethaneal tossed aside the
reins and stood up on the driver's bench waving his arms.

"Everyone! Stop what you're doing and gather around. Gather
around! I've urgent news you all must hear!" he called out after
his unexpected entrance. He made for quite a sight: He wore a
tight-fitting black shirt and wool trousers, his long golden hair
tied back from his handsome, angular face as he demanded their
attention.

Murmuring amongst themselves, the villagers stopped what
they were doing, the scattered conversations and the various
sounds of labor gradually becoming hushed. Almost cautiously,
they began to crowd in the street around the Dragon Slayer's
wagon.

"That's it, gather in, gather in. I've got an announcement
everyone needs to hear!" Nethaneal called out, waving in more
villagers from the back.

Alerted by the commotion, Urick emerged from the smithy's
tent where he'd been hard at work, frowning and wiping his sweaty
face and neck as he walked to the rear of the crowd gathered in
the street. Not far away Horris ducked out of the doorway of his
pub, crossing his thick arms over his barrel chest and waiting to

hear what the Dragon Slayer had to say.

Once satisfied he had enough of the villagers in attendance,
Nethaneal spread his arms wide and said, "Good news, everyone!
I stand before you now to announce that I am ready to slay the
dragon Temper!"

Nethaneal was hoping for at least a round of applause to
meet his announcement, if not a joyous outburst from the crowded
villagers. What he received, however, was entirely different:
Complete silence and empty, blinking eyes staring up at him. Two
chickens squabbled in the dirt nearby. Somewhere a donkey brayed.

Finally, a fat man screwed up his face into a curious
expression and asked, "An' just how the hell you plan on doin'
that?"

"Excellent question," Nethaneal said. He raised his voice
to announce to the rest of the crowd, "I have decided to
challenge Temper to a duel, just him and I. Tomorrow at sunrise
we will face one another in the field beyond the village.

This sent a murmur rippling throughout the crowd as the
villagers expressed their shock and disbelief.

One woman cupped her hands around her mouth and called out,
"Isn't there a better way? Your plan is madness!"

The gathering of villagers began calling out from different
parts of the crowd, voicing their support for this opinion. Not
only would such a foolhardy plan end in the Dragon Slayer's
immediate death, the villagers feared it would also bring
Temper's wrath down upon them for challenging his might.

Nethaneal lifted his hands to chest level, palms facing out, to calm them down. "Trust me! Please, trust me...I do not wish to die anymore than any of you," he explained, "But after much research I've learned that Temper is, at heart, a coward. He prefers to ambush his prey, terrorizing unsuspecting folk like you instead of facing a worthy opponent. That is why I've chosen to challenge Temper to a duel. Just him and I, while the entire village looks on. I will prove to you all that Temper is nothing but an oversized reptile, as capable of defeat as you or I."

The villagers shifted uneasily. Never before had they heard someone voice aloud such bold opinions about Temper. Just listening to the Dragon Slayer's challenging words made them feel uneasy, as though Temper could somehow overhear the conversation and would bring his wrath down upon them all.

"But there is one last thing I must ask," Nethaneal continued, "I need one of you, the bravest man here, to send word to Temper that I wish to challenge him."

"...You mean, **go** to Temper's castle and tell him you wish to duel?" a man asked, frowning as though he'd misheard.

Nethaneal pressed his palms together and smiled. "Yes. That's exactly what I mean."

The crowd of villagers reacted with instant consternation.

"Are yeh daft?" one man called out amid the aghast murmurs, "Yer askin' one of us to die!"

"No one's ever gone to Temper's lair and lived!"

"I ain't goin', yeh can count on that for damned sure!"

"There's nobody mad enough--"

"I'll do it," said a calm voice from the rear of the crowd.

Abruptly the jeers quieted as the villagers turned their heads to see who it was that was brave enough to volunteer for such a suicide mission.

There, standing slouched with his hands in his pants pockets, was Conner. His dark eyes scanning over the sea of stunned faces gawking at him, Conner repeated smugly, "I'll go to Temper and give him your challenge."

"Well I'll be damned...," someone uttered in the silence, dumbfounded that the scrawny rabbit farmer had any nerve about him.

Standing atop his wagon, Nethaneal shielded his eyes and squinted out over the crowd, feigning surprise when he saw Conner's dark hair and gaunt, pale face. "You there, you're willing to send my challenge to Temper?" he asked.

Conner forced a smile which only partially suppressed his disgusted sneer as he held the Dragon Slayer's gaze. "I am."

Nethaneal gestured to Conner with an exaggerated sweep of his arms for the benefit of the crowd. "And there you have it--A brave soul! Everyone, let's hear it for him, shall we?"

Still somewhat in shock, the villagers began to clap, slowly at first, and then all together as they realized what a sacrifice the scrawny young man was making. Several men even slapped him on the back to congratulate him on his bravery, realizing they had been wrong about the young man all along.

Conner simply smiled a tight, forced grin as he nodded his
head in acceptance of the praise, trying his best to conceal the
hatred and disgust he felt to be standing amongst these fools. He
couldn't wait to leave and tell Temper of the Dragon Slayer's
plan, and also of the villagers' collective support of it. Conner
would make sure that the next time Temper came to feed, no one
would dare question the dragon's might again. Then Maribel would
see how foolish she'd been to invest her trust in this pitiful
Dragon Slayer instead of him.

Once the applause had died out, Nethaneal said, "A great
welcome will be owed upon your return, Conner. I assure you
of this," Nethaneal said, still smiling handsomely.

"No need," Conner said with a slow smile which didn't match
the lecherous gleam in his dark eyes, "I'm...**happy**...to help."
Then he turned and began striding off, the amazed villagers
parting out of his way.

Nethaneal stood atop his wagon, watching Conner disappear
with a sort of sly, amused humor in his eyes. So far, everything
was going perfectly to plan.

Spotting Urick and Horris standing together amongst the
dispersing, still-murmuring crowd, Nethaneal leapt down off his
wagon and waved the two men over.

"So, yer really plannin' on followin' through with this, are
yeh?" Horris asked as he lumbered near.

"Too late to back out now," Nethaneal said, nodding towards
the edge of the village where Conner was already driving his cart

towards the tree line.

"How'd you know Conner would volunteer to send the challenge to Temper?" Urick asked, seeming to know something was afoot. No one in their right mind would venture within miles of the dragon's lair, and suddenly Conner, of all people, had volunteered to herald a challenge directly to Temper? It didn't add up. Obviously, Nethaneal knew something they didn't.

"He's a traitor," Nethaneal bluntly explained. "The day you took me to see Temper's castle, I watched him drive his cart up to the front gate and disappear inside. That's why I asked you who he was. He's on the side of the dragon."

"Now why would he do a thing like that?" Horris wondered.

"Maribel," Urick said, suddenly fitting the pieces together. It was so obvious: For the longest time Conner had had eyes for Maribel, so much so that Orion had seen it fit to scare him off anytime he came around. But would the scrawny rabbit farmer really stoop so low as to betray the entire village to the dragon simply because he felt threatened by Nethaneal? Because he was afraid Maribel would fall in love with him? Urick thought so. There had always been something sinister about the sneaky young man which had never set right with him.

Urick looked up from his thoughts at Nethaneal, realization of the situation sharpening his tired green eyes. "He wants you dead, Nethaneal."

Nethaneal simply shrugged. "I know."

"Why, that mangy little...," Horris growled, cracking his hairy knuckles. "I oughta run 'im down right now an' pummel his lyin' face into the dirt and--"

"Hold that thought, big man," Nethaneal told Horris as he continued to fume. "There will be plenty of time for that later. Right now I need help from the both of you."

"Alright," Horris said, bringing himself under control. He took a deep breath and asked, "Whatsit yeh need, Nethaneal?"

"I need you to round up a group of strong men, and as many shovels. Chains as well, as many as you can find. I'll also need four trees felled and limbed immediately. Time is of the essence."

Horris's thick brow furrowed, bewildered by the Dragon Slayer's odd requests. But, deciding Nethaneal knew what he was doing, Horris simply nodded his bald head and promptly replied, "Consider it done. Where yeh need us?"

"In the north end of the meadow. I'll meet you there to give you instructions."

"Right." With that, Horris lumbered off into the village determined to do his part in the plot to kill Temper.

"What do you need me to do?" Urick asked, eager to help.

"It's over here," Nethaneal said, tipping his head towards the rear of the wagon. There he pulled up the canvas flap, reached in, and with a labored grunt extracted a large iron harpoon which he held cradled in his arms. "I'm afraid this might not be sufficient for a dragon of Temper's size," he explained, hefting the harpoon in his arms. "I need the head of this widened and notched with barbs, if you could. Once I shoot Temper with it, it must stay buried in his flesh no matter how much he fights. If it doesn't hold, we'll all be in a tight spot."

Urick took the heavy iron harpoon from Nethaneal and hefted it in his hands. The head of it was flat and sharp, double-edged. The shaft was two feet long and as thick as a man's wrist, the entire thing weighing well over sixty pounds.

"I need it done before sunup. I would have asked you sooner, but I had to wait until Conner left the village. I couldn't risk him getting an idea of what I was up to," Nethaneal appologized.

Urick continued to examine the harpoon for a long moment, his hard green eyes tracing its length as if already imagining it buried in Temper's lifeless corpse. Then he rested the harpoon on his shoulder and fixed the Dragon Slayer with a stern, direct stare.

"I'll have it done," he said, "You just make sure it hits its mark."

## CHAPTER 27

Red sparks exploded off Urick's hammer as he stood over the coals, flattening a length of iron in his workshop. Already past nightfall, he labored by the wavering glow of a pair of lanterns, the interior of his cluttered workspace lit a diluted red by the glowing coals. As he worked, beads of sweat rolled down Urick's roughly determined face, dripping off his chin and hissing off the glowing iron in short-lived slivers of steam. Cords of muscle strained in his thick forearms, his hammer emitting a continuous series of ping-ping-pings, the sparks flaring from each impact blazing in his eyes as he stood in the shimmering hot air.

He'd had enough. Too many times Urick had been forced to hide in the trees like a frightened animal as Temper wreaked havoc upon his village, forced to listen helplessly to the screams of his fellow villagers being eaten alive, forced to watch as their homes burned to the ground amid the dragon's flames.

Ten years ago he'd lost his beloved wife Charlotte to Temper. Now he'd lost his son Orion. Who would be next to fall victim to Temper's wrath? Maribel? Horris? Himself?

Urick bared his clenched teeth as he pounded the glowing iron with his hammer, the sparks flaring as red as rage in his eyes.

He'd lived in constant fear of Temper for years now. Countless nights he'd spent laying awake in bed, praying to the Gods that his family would be spared the dragon's torments. Too many times his startled gaze had been drawn skyward at the hint of a fleeting shadow, only to find that a cloud had passed in front of the sun. Urick was tired of living in fear of Temper, with the shame and regret that came with being a man who was entirely helpless to protect his own family from danger. He was tired of visiting the empty graves of his wife and son every evening after supper, promising things would be set right some day, but knowing in his heart that he was helpless to avenge their deaths.

No more.

Tossing his hammer aside, Urick picked up a bucket of water and poured it over the harpoon, the water billowing into steam as it hissed off the hot iron. Then Urick set the bucket aside and mopped his brow with a rag, examining his work.

He's done just as Nethaneal had requested. He'd widened the twin blades of the harpoon's head, notching its steepled edges

with barbs so that when the harpoon punched into the dragon's
flesh it would remain anchored in place. The iron had bonded
seamlessly to the existing metal, as strong as if the harpoon had
been forged in one solid piece.

But it wasn't quite done.

While studying the harpoon, a grim idea suddenly came to
Urick. Deciding to follow through on it, Urick turned away from
the workbench, picked up one of his lanterns, and ducked out of
the smithy.

Outside, the village was dimly illuminated by the half-moon
shining through the scattered tufts of black clouds above, its
silver-blue glow cast down onto the serrated ridges of thatch-
roofed huts.

His bootheels crunching in the silence of the dirt street,
Urick made his way to the north end of the village and started
out across the meadow. As the quietly hissing blades of grass
parted before him, Urick glanced to the west end of the meadow
where dozens of glowing, disembodied lanterns floated in the
distant shadows amid muffled sounds of labor as the villagers
worked through the night to help the Dragon Slayer prepare for
his duel with Temper.

Coming to the edge of the looming black forest, Urick knelt
down beside Orion's grave, setting the softly glowing lantern
beside the small pile of stones.

"Forgive me Orion...but I know you would have wanted this,"
Urick said quietly. He then leaned forward, dismantled the pile
of stones, and began raking away the rich black soil. Soon he

unearthed the dagger Orion had crafted, tenderly wiping the blade
clean on the thigh of his trousers and blowing it off before
picking up his lantern and striding off into the meadow.

Back in the red glow of his workshop's interior, Urick
raised his hammer above his head, and with one powerful strike
broke the blade of Orion's dagger off at the handle. Tossing
aside the handle, Urick picked up the blade with a pair of tongs
and buried it in the bed of glowing hot coals. Then he began
working the bellows, his vein-laced arms bulging as he pumped air
over the coals with a methodical hiss-wheeze, their angry red
glow flaring to white beneath the intense heat.

After a time Urick used the tongs to retrieve the red-hot
blade from the coals and place it on his workbench. There he
aligned a straight-blade chisel to the center of the blade and
struck the end of it with his hammer, repeating this process
several more times until the blade had been split up the middle
in the shape of a V. Once done, Urick again returned to split
blade to the coals to heat.

After the metal had softened enough, he used the tongs to
carefully place the blade over the tip of the harpoon and
hammered it flat. Finally he poured a measure of water over the
harpoon and held it up to inspect his work, steam hissing past
his hardened, soot-streaked face.

The blade of Orion's dagger now capped the point of the
harpoon's tip, gleaming sharply in the coal's red glow. It was
ready.

Orion's blade had tasted Temper's blood before, and Urick would see to it that it did so again.

CHAPTER 28

By the glowing orb of his lantern, Conner made his way
through the overgrown courtyard and into Temper's castle, which
loomed against the starry night sky like a jagged black mountain.
Fearless with purpose, he strode down the cavernous hallway, the
dry creek of his lantern's handle and the clunk of his bootheels
echoing distantly off the towering stone walls.

Irritated by the intrusion into their world of darkness,
sleek black cockroaches scurried across the dusty marble floors
away from the glow of Conner's lantern like hundreds of fleeing
shadows. Mangy rats hissed as they darted behind cobweb-draped
statues and rusted armor, leaning out with their teeth bared and
their black eyes gleaming hatefully to watch as Conner strode
past in the dark corridor. In the vast expanse of darkness within
the castle bats chittered and swooped with the leathery flap of
little wings, the bluish rays of moonlight slanting in from the

shattered windows above capturing their fleeting silhouettes for only an instant before they vanished.

Conner hurried his way up the sweeping marble staircase, only feeling his first creeping tingle of apprehension as he came to the open doors of the dragon's chambers. But then he took in a deep breath, reminding himself again that he was doing this in order to kill the Dragon Slayer and win back Maribel. Steeling himself with this thought, Conner let out the breath he'd been holding and strode into the arched doorway.

At the far end of the expansive chamber, two ruby red eyes slid open in the darkness.

"Conner...," Temper's deep voice rumbled. The looming stained-glass windows through which the bluish moonlight shone created an imposing silhouette as Temper raised his massive horned head at the end of his long, serpentine neck. "What brings you here, at this hour, to disturb my rest?" Temper demanded from atop his nest of gold treasures.

His hand trembling so severely that his lantern rattled as he walked the length of the hall, Conner dropped to a knee and servilely bowed his head to the dragon. "Temper, your Greatness, I've--I've come to bring word of the Dragon Slayer, as you have ordered me."

"What is it?" Temper inquired, his attention aroused.

His head still bowed in fear, Conner explained, "The Dragon Slayer has challenged you to a duel, mighty Temper. This morning, at sunrise, he will be waiting for you in the meadow beyond the village." Conner tilted back his head to look up at Temper, a

sour look of contempt sharpening his gaunt face into a sneer
illuminated by the wavering glow of his lantern. "He slanders
your name publicly, great Temper."

Temper's eyes narrowed to blood-red slits. Scaled lips
peeling back from his jagged teeth, the dragon growled, "What
does he say?"

"Horrible things"--Conner's eyes darted uncomfortably--
"Rebellious. Obscene. He...He calls you a coward, mighty Temper.
He told the villagers you wouldn't face a worthy opponent such as
him and survive."

Temper's hooked claws flexed with anger, chipping deep ruts
into the marble floor before him as a murderous growl rumbled
deep within his scaled body.

"There's more," Conner continued, "The villagers applauded
his words, mighty Temper. They cheered. He's got them all
convinced he can kill you. The entire village will be gathered in
the forest at sunrise to witness the duel."

"All the better!" snarled Temper, the yellow flames licking
through his teeth flash-lighting the dark chamber. "That way they
can watch me tear their Dragon Slayer limb from limb before I
devour them as well. After tomorrow, none will dare utter my name
for fear of the blood that I am about to spill!" The sheer force
behind Temper's furious words shook the very foundation of the
castle, dust sifting down from the cavernous ceiling above.

A lecherous smile spreading slowly across his pale face in
the glow of his lantern as he remembered how he'd sabotaged

Nethaneal's weapon, Conner said, "I have faith you will, **great**

**Temper**."

CHAPTER 29


"Everyone, get to cover! Hurry--**HURRY!**" Nethaneal yelled as
he stood in the meadow.

While the golden halo of the nascent morning sun was just
beginning to crest the horizon, scattered groups of peasants were
fleeing the village and hurrying across the meadow towards the
cover of forest, trying to get to safety before Temper arrived.
Some men carried armloads of possessions they wished to protect
from the dragon's fire, while most were more concerned with
ushering their wives, children, and the elderly into the safety
of the trees.

"Don't worry about the animals, they can fend for
themselves. Just go!" Nethaneal said, waving the villagers past.
It was of the utmost importance they get to cover before Temper
arrived. Nethaneal's plan was already dangerous enough without

putting anyone else in harm's way.

Just then Horris, his clothes soiled with dirt, lumbered up
to Nethaneal wiping the sweat from his bald head and panted,
"Me an' the boys just finished up. Didja need anything else
done?"

"No, that was all," Nethaneal said, relief flooding his
system that the workers had finished the preparations in time.
"You just get to safety with the others. I'll handle the rest."

Horris clapped Nethaneal on the shoulder with a huge hand,
nodding his approval as he looked the Dragon Slayer up and down.
"Yer alright, yeh know that? Yeh be careful."

"I'm a Dragon Slayer," Nethaneal said, his blue eyes hard
with humorous determination, "You're not paying me to be careful.
Now go."

Horris grinned wide, revealing his missing front tooth, and
nodded his sincere approval once more before picking up his
shovel and heading towards the treeline with the other workers.

Once the last of the villagers had retreated into the cover
of the trees and left him standing alone in the meadow, Nethaneal
shrugged off his coat and tossed it aside as he strode quickly
over to his cannon. Underneath he wore a dark pair of trousers
tucked into heavy boots and a tight-fitting shirt, his golden
hair tied back out of his face. On a leather belt around his
waist he wore a long sword just in case there were complications
with the cannon. He prayed there wouldn't be; a sword was a
pathetic weapon against a dragon such as Temper, but it was

better than nothing.

Glancing to the east just as the early sun broke over the horizon in an explosion of golden rays, Nethaneal hurriedly loaded the cannon with a cloth powder charge, pushing it down the barrel with the ramrod. Then he slid the harpoon into the barrel so that only its barbed, gleaming tip was visible. A thick chain was attached to the harpoon's end, extending down to a tall coil of chain partially hidden in the grass.

Nethaneal was making his way around to the back of the cannon when he heard a woman's voice suddenly cry out his name. Alerted, he straightened up and saw that Maribel had left the cover of the forest and was running through the tall grass towards him, the hem of her dress held in her hands, her long brown hair flowing.

"Maribel?" he said, "What are you doing out here? Get back to cover!"

Maribel stopped before him, nervous anxiety tightening her smooth, beautiful face. Hastily, she said, "I...I need to tell you something before you do this, Nethaneal."

"Now's not the time, Maribel," Nethaneal said, his blue eyes distractedly scanning across the early morning sky, "You need to get to safety with the others. Temper will be here any--"

Nethaneal was caught entirely by surprise when Maribel suddenly grabbed him by the front of his shirt, stood up on her toes, and pressed her soft lips to his in a long, warm, drawn-out kiss. When it ended Nethaneal opened his eyes, shocked to realize that for that one brief moment while Maribel's lips were pressed to his, he'd completely forgotten all about Temper and their coming battle.

"Good luck, Nethaneal," Maribel said as she lowered herself back down, looking both worried over his safety and embarrassed about what she'd just done. Across the meadow the crowd of villagers packed amongst the trees craned their necks as they looked on, wondering what was going on between the two.

Nethaneal cleared his throat, the sun's rays dazzling all around them. "Thank you, Maribel," he managed to say as he stared down into her bright green eyes. Then his sense of urgency returned in a flash, wrenching him from the euphoric moment and back into the present. "Now go hide!" he said, ushering her away.

With one last nervous, bashful smile, Maribel turned and ran across the meadow into the dense treeline with the rest of the villagers. There she crouched down behind the trunk of a giant elm beside her father, who, having watched the entire encounter, glanced sidelong down at his daughter.

Noticing her father's critical stare, Maribel looked at him and said incredulously, "What? It was for good luck."

Urick merely grunted and returned to watching the sky for Temper, knowing full well there had been much, much more behind that kiss than a mere good luck wish.

With the first pulses of adrenaline beginning to course through his body, Nethaneal bent down and picked up the lanyard protruding from the rear of the cannon. Looping the leather strap

around his fist, he straightened up with his jaw clenched
readily, ears atune, eyes scanning the morning sky for signs of
the dragon.

Now was the time.

There was no turning back now.

As Nethaneal stood waiting behind his cannon, lanyard in
hand, a fresh morning breeze swayed over the meadow, blowing a
strand of golden hair off his brow. The sun had fully cleared the
serrated ridge of mountains in the east...But **where** was Temper?

Nethaneal's blue eyes narrowed as he turned in a circle,
impatiently awaiting the dragon's arrival, searching the light
morning skyline for signs of movement.

A long moment of fearful silence passed. At the forest's
edge dozens of villagers looked on in tense anticipation, their
faces, old and young alike, anxiously peering out from behind
trees, limbs, and shrubs.

Something didn't feel right.

Then a shadow fell over the land, in an instant casting the
bright morning sunlight into darkness.

CHAPTER 30

Temper cut a fearsome silhouette against the morning sky as
he banked in the air, the sunlight flashing past his gigantic
wings as he made one full revolution in the sky above like a
colossal bird of prey circling its victims.

The villagers cowering in the forest gasped with fright at
the sight of the coming dragon and withdrew behind mossy
boulders, logs, and trees in order to stay hidden from danger.
Several women screamed. Children began to cry as they hid their
faces in their hands.

Temper banked in the air and came sweeping down out of the
sky, landing in the meadow forty paces ahead of Nethaneal with a
ground shaking impact, the cushioning beat of his huge wings so
powerful it flattened the tall grass all around him.

Standing behind his cannon with the lanyard held in his

hand, Nethaneal took a deep, steadying breath and said to himself, "Big one."

Everything he'd heard about Temper had been true, if not understated. The dragon had the sheer size and brilliant green coloring of a Night-Bringing Colossus, its body the size of a ship, its neck and tail each as long and thick as pine trees. The dragon's head was diamond-shaped, like a viper's, with two fearsome horns sweeping from up off its brow. Its red eyes were slitted and nearly aglow in the early sunlight, the vicious resemblance to a Plague-Tongued Death Reaper subtle yet unmistakable.

At that instant, Nethaneal knew he was looking at the deadliest dragon he'd ever faced.

Snarling murderously, Temper reared back his head and bared his razor-sharp rows of teeth, his jade scales flaring menacingly along his flanks. "Is it you who dares challenge **me**?" he demanded in a fierce roar, the searing heat of his breath shimmering the cool morning air.

Terrified, the villagers cowering in the forest held their breath as they watched the confrontation. If the Dragon Slayer's plan failed, Temper would no doubt wreak havoc on their village again, killing all whom he suspected of supporting the Dragon Slayer in this mutony. All they could do was watch and pray.

Nethaneal stood his ground behind his cannon, staring up at the monstrous beast poised ready to attack just yards away. Although his heart was racing and adrenaline was coursing like

fire through his veins, Nethaneal kept his chiseled face stony
and unreadable. Dragons such as Temper thrived on the fear they
instilled in others, were attracted to it like predators to the
scent of blood. The only way to keep Temper off balance was to
rattle him, to manipulate his pride and force him into making a
mistake.

To do this, Nethaneal flashed a pleasant smile and offered
Temper a small bow from the waist, one arm extended. "It is I--
Nethaneal Morris, at your service. And I assume that you're..."
He looked around as if having forgotten the dragon's name, then
squinted curiously and asked, "Tantrum, isn't it?"

"**I-AM-TEMPER!**" the colossal dragon roared, twin bursts of
flame blasting from his nostrils.

"My apologies, great Temper," Nethaneal said with a
conceding smile, uncowered by the dragon's show of ferocity. "I'm
awful with names. You see, I've killed so many of your kind over
the years that I can no longer remember their names. Nothing
personal, I assure you. It's just that you all look so much alike
to me."

Temper's black forked tongue slithered out from between his
rows of bared teeth, venomous saliva glistening off his fangs.
His slitted, reptilian eyes shifted from Nethaneal to the forest
edge. There he could see the faces of the dozens of villagers
peering fearfully from out around the trees to watch the
confrontation. After he was finished slaughtering this fool, they
would all pay dearly for this insurrection--They had seen **nothing**

yet!

Fixing his attention back onto the Dragon Slayer, Temper growled, "I have slaughtered whole armies and toppled kingdoms. And now you, one lone man, dare stand before me?"

Nethaneal made it a point to glance casually back over each shoulder before looking back up at Temper. He shrugged. "It would appear so, wouldn't it?"

Inwardly, Nethaneal was calculating the distance between himself and the dragon. Because of the meadow's tall grass it was difficult to notice, but there was an area of disturbed earth between himself and Temper--the results of the workers' labors throughout the night. In order for his plan to work effectively, Nethaneal had to lure Temper close to that mark. If he misjudged, a bloody death for him as well as the villagers would quickly follow. He would only have one chance.

Temper's slit-pupiled eyes shifted to the odd wheeled contraption the Dragon Slayer stood behind. "Do you really think that weapon will harm **me**?" he demanded, beginning to stalk forward through the grass on low, powerful haunches.

"No," Nethaneal said, his intense blue eyes shifting between the advancing dragon and the disturbed area of ground. Almost there...almost... "No, this weapon will **kill** you. You see, dragons such as yourself aren't long for this world, Temper. Humankind is reclaiming our lands. Now, you can either admit defeat before all watching here and depart with your life, or I can blow you to bloody shreds. It's your choice."

Flames licked through Temper's bared fangs, blazing hotly in his eyes as he continued to advance on the human who had the audacity to speak to him in such a reckless fashion.

"I am immortal!" Temper roared, the power of his voice echoing like thunder off the mountains. "Amongst the legions of dragons born to fire, I alone reign supreme! And over humans, I am a God! I can crush this land, and all in it as I see fit."

The monstrous dragon then reared back on his hind legs to his full towering height, brazenly revealing the pale, plated scales of his underbelly. "Strike your first blow, **human!**" he snarled the challenge, about to show everyone watching what would happen when the coals of his rage were stoked.

"As you wish," Nethaneal said with a deadly smirk, knowing he'd manipulated Temper's ego into playing directly into his trap.

Then Nethaneal jerked the lanyard.

## CHAPTER 31

**BOOM!** Nethaneal's cannon bucked with a violent thunderclap
of gray smoke.

The gleaming-tipped harpoon was shot from the cannon's
barrel and sent hurtling through the air, the length of chain
attached to its end rattling as it whipped off the spool coiled
in the grass. Then the harpoon slammed into Temper's brazenly
exposed chest, shattering his scales upon impact and biting into
the dragon's flesh. The impact was enough to knock the dragon
back down onto all fours--but little more.

Enraged to find a harpoon buried in his chest and surprised
by the deep throb of pain it had brought, Temper bared his teeth
in a fiery snarl, slitted pupils narrowing in his red eyes as he
whipped his horned head around to face his enemy. Temper had
merely been toying with this man for his own amusement, but now

realized it was unwise to continue this game. This mortal did in
fact possess a formidable weapon to have penetrated his thick
scales, and Temper decided he would eliminate this Dragon Slayer,
here and now!

Releasing a roar which seemed to shake the very earth to its
core, Temper unfolded his massive wings at his sides and launched
himself into the air.

Nethaneal saw the dragon take to the air and begin coming
straight at him, fearsome mouth stretched wide, huge wings
flattening the grass and swirling the gray cannon smoke lingering
in the air with each beat. The cannon shot hardly seemed to have
affected the monstrous dragon.

Cursing under his breath, Nethaneal ran around to the front
of the cannon, lowered his shoulder to its smoking barrel, and
with a labored bellow began to push it backwards through the
grass in an attempt to put distance between himself and the
attacking dragon.

"Nethaneal!" Maribel screamed in horror as she rushed to the
forest's edge, watching helplessly as the dragon closed in on
him from across the meadow, "BEHIND YOU!"

Temper's scaled lips peeled back from his gleaming, poison-
slickened teeth as he swept down out of the sky, hooked talons
flashing open, mere seconds from pouncing on the foolish mortal
and tearing him to shreds--

Suddenly the chain attached to the harpoon in Temper's chest
snapped taunt. This chain met four others, which were each

anchored to the logs the men had buried deep in the meadow the night before. Temper's yawning jaws were just feet from closing over Nethaneal when these chains reached their length with a resounding CLACK!, jerking Temper from the sky and sending him crashing into the meadow in a monstrous heap of scales, flapping wings, and slashing talons.

Nethaneal gave his cannon one last shove back and turned around to see the dragon furiously trying to right itself, roaring flame, beating its wings and wildly thrashing its tail.

"I got you now, you son of a bitch!" Nethaneal said, his blue eyes alight with the raw thrill of battle. He had Temper just where he wanted him.

But as Temper got to his feet and again turned his malicious reptilian gaze onto him, Nethaneal saw that there was already a problem: The harpoon, which should have been buried clear to the hilt in Temper's chest, had barely penetrated past the tips of its blade, leaving the entire shaft exposed. Because of this, the harpoon was hanging from the dragon's bleeding chest at a loose angle, its barbs the only thing keeping its purchase in Temper's flesh.

It wouldn't hold for long.

Lacking the time to figure out why his cannon suddenly lacked power, Nethaneal bent down and hurriedly picked up a pouch of black powder from the pile of pre-made charges he'd placed on the ground there earlier. Nethaneal had measured the length of the chain and paced off enough distance between its end and

himself so that once he had the dragon anchored, he could shoot
it with his cannon at a safe distance.

Tearing the cloth pouch with his teeth, Nethaneal used the
ramrod to stuff the charge to the rear of the cannon, packing it
tight against the primer. Then he withdrew the ramrod, loaded in
a cannonball, and rushed around to the rear of the cannon.

Temper had just begun his second charge, teeth snapping,
talons ripping away chunks of earth, when Nethaneal lined up his
shot and jerked the lanyard with another thunderclap explosion.
The cannonball struck Temper high on the shoulder and glanced
off, ripping away a gory path of scales. It was a shot that
should have resulted in far more damage than a mere flesh wound.
**What** the hell was the matter?

Temper roared furiously and kept charging, unmindful of the
pain. Again the chains anchored in the meadow snapped taunt, and
like a rabid dog at the end of its tether the dragon slashed his
claws and gnashed his teeth, straining to reach Nethaneal who
stood only yards away.

Nethaneal was rushing to reload the cannon, heart hammering
with adrenaline, when the monstrous dragon suddenly reared back.
Blood spattered flanks expanding as he inhailed, Temper then
opened his fearsome maw and roared an intense column of blue-
orange flame down at Nethaneal.

"Damn!" Nethaneal cursed, diving to the ground and covering
the black powder charges with his body to protect them from the
flame. Not a second later the dragon's fire rolled across the

meadow in a churning wave of flame that instantly incinerated the tall grass.

Laying face-down on the ground, Netheaneal felt the searing heat wash over him, burning his flesh like acid. The pain was excruciating. Nethaneal clenched his jaw and bellowed through his teeth, forcing himself to lay still despite the pain. If he allowed the fire to touch the charges he would be blown sky-high and the villagers would be left to deal with Temper's wrath. Nethaneal **would not** let that happen.

After what seemed like an eternity of unbearable pain, the wave of fire rolled past. Nethaneal leapt to his feet and tore off his burning shirt, his muscled back bright red with blistered burns. Ignoring the pain, Nethaneal picked up a steaming hot cannonball and loaded it into the barrel. The meadow around him was now a blackened, fire-strewn stage, red embers swirling on the air. Temper was attempting to tear the harpoon out of his chest, roaring with pain as the barbs tore his flesh, when Nethaneal again fired the cannon.

This time the heavy iron ball punched against the side of the dragon's thick neck, whipping his head to the side and tearing away a deep rut of flesh with a misty explosion of blood.

Nethaneal couldn't believe what he was seeing through the swirling smoke and embers. That blow should have nearly decapitated the dragon!

Temper recovered from the painful blow, flecks of blood now staining his teeth as he again lunged for Nethaneal, hooked talons slashing like a lion's claws through the air. The harpoon strained to hold the monstrous dragon back, the barbs slipping out another notch from his flesh.

Again Temper reared back, stretching open his fearsome mouth to roar a column of flame down at the mortal--

Nothing happened.

Temper only managed to release a strangled, gurgling roar, producing just a small blast of flame and a gush of blood. Unaccustomed to experiencing pain during battle, Temper shook his horned head and again stretched open his terrible mouth to roar fire. This time the dragon succeeded in producing only more blood which flowed nightmarishly out from between his razor-sharp teeth.

Despite not having its desired effect, Nethaneal realized the cannonball had managed to rupture something in the dragon's neck, rendering its flame useless. Encouraged by the small victory, Nethaneal hurriedly loaded the cannon and again lined up his shot.

**BOOM!**

The cannonball streaked through the air and struck the dragon broadside, ripping a hole in its wing and cleaving away a large patch of scales down its flank. Temper roared with pain and tried to retaliate, but was held anchored in place by the chained harpoon bured in his chest.

Nethaneal was relentless. Working with practiced efficiency, he again loaded the cannon and took aim.

Temper was again attempting to rip the harpoon out of his chest when Nethaneal jerked back on the lanyard, the cannon bucking a fourth time. This time the cannonball sailed high, striking the dragon in the face with the force to shatter both horns off its brow and violently whip back its head. Fazed by the blow, the monstrous dragon staggered back on shaky haunches, bleeding head lolling defenselessly.

The villagers huddled in the forest gasped and covered their mouths with trembling hands as they watched Temper collapse to the ground, hoping the dragon was about to die.

They were sorely disappointed.

Horns shattered, wings torn, blood leaking steadily from his face, mouth, chest, and flanks, Temper shook his head and snarled as he regained his bearings, the black pupils in his ruby-red eyes narrowing to a razor's edge. Driven mad by furious bloodlust, the dragon reared back and clutched the harpoon buried in its chest, and with an ungodly roar of defiance, wrenched the harpoon out of its flesh, snapping the thick chain which had been anchoring him into place.

"...No," Nethaneal uttered.

This, Nethaneal knew at that moment, was about to get difficult.

Throwing the harpoon aside, Temper dropped down onto all fours and began advancing across the meadow like a predator stalking its prey. "Fool!" the dragon snarled with his diamond-shaped head held low, blood leaking in numerous rivulets from between his sharp teeth, "Only death comes to those who challenge me!"

Knowing he only had seconds to act before the gargantuan dragon was upon him, Nethaneal scooped up a cannonball and hurriedly loaded it into the barrel. Then he ran around to the rear of the cannon, looped his hand through the lanyard, and pulled--

Too late.

Temper roared and spun in a half-circle, whipping his log-thick tail around so fast that Nethaneal never saw it coming. The impact slapped the cannon aside like a toy just as it went off with a booming report, the cannonball crashing harmlessly into the trees. Nethaneal was sent airborne at the same moment, the wind crushed from his lungs. He hit the ground some distance away and slid to a stop, eyelids fluttering.

Not far away Temper licked his bloody teeth with his forked tongue as he stalked across the burning meadow, the swirling embers gleaming evilly in his red eyes. He had suffered far too much pain and embarrassment at the hands of this mortal and his annoying weapon, and was about to put an end to this mutiny once and for all. And after he was finished with the Dragon Slayer, Temper would turn his wrath on the villagers for believing that he--the most powerful dragon in all the land--could possibly be slain by a common mortal.

His brain throbbing in his skull, Nethaneal managed to open his eyes, his blurred vision gradually coming into focus. What he

saw snapped him back to reality with a sudden jolt of alarm:
Temper's viper-shaped head looming over him, horns shattered,
blood leaking from between his narrowed red eyes, crimson-
streaked fangs bared in a nightmarish snarl of hunger. And as
Nethaneal watched, Temper lifted one of his forepaws, hooked
talons flashing open like razors in murderous anticipation.

Nethaneal cursed and kicked his legs up over his head,
rolling over backwards just as Temper slashed at him, talons
ripping three deep ruts into the soil.

Leaping to his feet, Nethaneal was left with no other option
but to draw his sword. If this was the way he would be forced to
battle the dragon, then so be it.

"Just you and me now!" he yelled challengingly up at the
dragon, the bulging muscles in his arms, chest, and stomach
flexing readily as he held the gleaming blade in both hands.

Temper growled deep in his throat at the Dragon Slayer's
unnerving lack of fear, blood bubbles sizzling from between his
interlocked teeth. Outraged that he'd had this much trouble
battling one petty human, Temper arched his neck and struck at
Nethaneal, intent on ripping him in half.

Nethaneal saw the strike coming and spun to the right, to
the side of the dragon's wounded neck. With a bellow of rage he
sank his sword into the dragon's gaping wound and twisted the
blade unmercifully.

The dragon roared with pain and pulled away, a gush of blood
spurting from its wound and splattering hotly against Nethaneal's

chest.

Thrilled by the savage feeling of the dragon's lifeblood on his skin, Nethaneal leapt away and hacked his sword across Temper's wing, opening a long gash in the leathery flesh.

Temper responded by flapping open the injured wing, knocking Nethaneal off balance. Before he could recover Temper spun and viciously slashed his talons through the air.

"AAAAGH!" Nethaneal bellowed, his sword spinning away and disappearing into the flames of the burning meadow. He stumbled back clutching his left arm, which had been torn open from shoulder to wrist by one of the dragon's razor-sharp talons and was leaking a continuous stream of blood from a severed artery.

Temper closed in on the Dragon Slayer, his slitted pupils dilating with anticipation as he scented the human's pungent blood on the hot, smoke-filled air. "This ends now!" Temper hissed, gnashing his bloody teeth.

Exhausted, wounded, and bleeding profusely, the two stood facing one another in the burning meadow, hissing flames dancing all around them while hot embers drifted past on the wind. And for that one brief mement the two were no longer human and dragon, but rather two warriors, equal in savagery, facing one another for the final battle.

His sweat-sheened face scorched and blood-spattered, Nethaneal clutched his arm to help stem the flow of blood as he stood fearlessly before the dragon. If he was about to die, he sure as hell wouldn't give this monster the satisfaction of showing the slightest amount of fear before it happened.

His blue eyes blazing with defiance, Nethaneal said, "It might be over for me, Temper. But I can guarantee it's just begun for you."

"How so, **human**?" Temper demanded as he stalked forward, his red eyes flashing in the firelight, head held low, spikes bristling along the ridge of his back.

Despite his nearly severed arm, Nethaneal laughed as he watched the fearsome dragon close in on him. "Look at yourself! You're wounded, Temper. You're **bleeding**," he said mockingly. "Everyone watching now knows you're capable of defeat. You're not a God. You're an overgrown lizard, as mortal as the rest of us. Just like the rest of your kind that I've slain." Nethaneal chuckled again, his face beginning to pale from bloodloss as syrupy beads of crimson continued to drip from the fingers of his wounded arm. "How long do you think you'll last when word of this spreads, hmm? Me, one lone man, tore you to shreds. Don't you see? Even if you kill me now, I've still won. I've broken the fear you've held over this land, and now hundreds--thousands--of men just like me are going to hunt you down. We're coming, I assure you. And it doesn't look to me that you're in any shape to stop us."

Smiling with brazen defiance at the dragon's fate, Nethaneal raised his arms out to his sides, inviting the dragon to deliver his death blow. "Go ahead, **mighty** Temper. Mine will be the last blood you'll ever taste. You'd better enjoy it."

Infuriated beyond anything he had ever experienced, Temper
reared back, scales bristling, his bared fangs gleaming with
blood and venom. The monstrous dragon released a chilling roar
and struck, intent on tearing the irksome human limb from limb--

"**Die, you monster!**" a man's voice suddenly rang out.

Materializing from out of the swirling flames of the burning
meadow, Urick came running forward wielding a pitchfork while
emitting a roaring battle cry. Leaping high into the air, he
raised the pitchfork over his head like a spear and drove it deep
into the bleeding wound on Temper's flank.

Temper's jaws were mere inches from closing over Nethaneal
when the dragon roared with pain and whipped his head to the
side, finding yet another pestering human foolish enough to
challenge him. The Dragon Slayer momentarily forgotten, Temper
was turning to dispatch of this newest annoyance when a stone
sailed high through the air and pelted off his muzzle. Shaking
off the blow, Temper saw that a third human--this one a woman--
had joined the others in their revolt.

"Go back to hell, you demon!" Maribel screamed as she stood
in the burning meadow. Tears were streaking her furious face as
she again pulled back her arm and hurled another stone at the
monstrous dragon.

Before Temper could decide which one of these nagging humans
to kill first, yet another joined the fight.

"TAKE **THIIIIIS!**" Horris bellowed. The giant bald man came
running through a wall of flame, ax held high, and with an

awesome surge of strength sank the weapon into the dragon's
hindquarters.

Temper snarled with pain and whipped his powerful tail,
batting Horris nearly fifty feet back through the air.

It was as if a dam broke.

In one massive wave the villagers who'd been cowering in the
forest suddenly broke cover and came flooding across the meadow
with a collective battle cry. Years of pain, fear, anguish, and
oppression suddenly igniting into murderous revolt, the
villagers, men and women alike, came charging through the flames
of the burning meadow. Armed with pitchforks, swords, shovels,
axes, and picks, they attacked the dragon in a swarm of furious
bodies.

Temper tried to roar flame at the sea of attacking villagers
closing in all around him, but again produced nothing but a
steaming jet of hot blood.

One scrawny man leapt onto Temper's back and, screaming like
a berserker, sank a pick between the dragon's scales. Another man
slashed his sword across Temper's already tattered wing, opening
up another gash.

Temper snarled and struck blindly at the sea of smaller
bodies surrounding him, plucking a man off the ground and tearing
him in two with a vicious shake of his head.

"Get him! GET HIM!" Maribel screamed amongst the rioting
crowd of bodies as she continued to hurl stones at the snarling,
slashing, roaring dragon.

A half dozen men were piled onto Temper's thick tail, trying to pin it down beneath their weight. It didn't work: With a fierce whip of his tail Temper sent the men flying, cartwheeling through the air. But the villagers wouldn't be stopped. Seeing the dragon wounded, fireless, and vulnerable, they knew this would be their one and only chance to kill the dragon which had for so long victimized them. They surrounded the beast in a violent swarm, hacking unmercifully into its exposed wounds with shovels and axes.

Temper slashed several villagers down with his sharp talons before roaring with pain as a man rammed a spear into one of his exposed cannonball wounds. The dragon wheeled around in desperation, biting, slashing, sweeping his tail indiscriminately into the sea of bodies in a futile attempt to fight them off. But still the villagers charged, undeterred and blind with fury.

For the first time in his entire life, Temper knew fear. Realizing he had to get away or he'd be overwhelmed by the villagers in his weakened, injured state, Temper unfolded his massive wings, throwing dozens of the attacking villagers skyward. Rearing back onto his hindquarters, Temper started to beat his wings. But the many ragged holes torn in his leathery flesh by the cannonballs and the villagers' weapons made it difficult to create any lift, each beat of his wings raising him only several feet higher into the air.

"Don't let the bastard get away!" Horris yelled, his nose bleeding profusely as he raced forward and jumped into the air, wrapping the end of the dragon's tail in a tight bear hug.

Still the villagers attacked as Temper began to raise into the air above them, hurling their weapons and screaming nasty insults up at the wounded dragon.

"Damnit!" Horris yelled as he was lifted higher and higher above the meadow while clinging to the dragon's tail. Realizing his weight wasn't enough to hold the dragon down, he decided with a curse to let go while he still could, dropping fifteen feet down through the air and crashing heavily to the ground.

Seeing that the dragon was about to escape their clutches despite the villagers' collective efforts to bring it down, Urick paused in the midst of the chaos and glanced around, searching desperately for some way to stop Temper once and for all.

It was then that he saw it through the wall of frantic bodies: The overturned cannon, the pile of unused charges, and the discarded harpoon which Temper had torn out of his own chest.

Knowing what he had to do, Urick began to shove his way back through the crowd of villagers still hurling objects up at Temper, yelling, "Get out of my way! MOVE! **MOVE!**"

Running as fast as he could, Urick broke free from the crowd and sprinted across the blackened, burning meadow. There he hurriedly gathered up all six of the remaining cloth pouches filled with black powder and ran them to the overturned cannon. He dropped the charges, bent down, and with a strained bellow lifted the side of the heavy cannon and tipped it back onto its wheels.

Frantically trying to recall Nethaneal's words from the first day he'd arrived to the village and explained how the strange contraption worked, Urick tore open one of the charges and pushed it into the barrel with his arm. Not quite sure if that would be enough, Urick decided to load the rest of the charges into the cannon one after the other until all of them were gone. Lastly he ran to retrieve the bloody harpoon laying nearby and loaded it into the barrel. His face sheened with sweat, Urick then hurried around to the rear of the cannon and glanced skyward.

Temper was getting away.

The dragon, wounded and raining sheets of blood in a macabre downpouring from his many wounds, had risen nearly a hundred feet into the sky and was flying unsteadily over the village with labored beats of his torn, injured wings.

Knowing he would have only one chance at this, Urick grabbed the cannon's wheels and forced them in opposite directions, turning the cannon to line up his shot. Then he tilted back the barrel, estimating as best he could what the trajectory of the harpoon and Temper's direction of flight would be.

This was his only hope.

Clutching the lanyard in his fist, his green eyes hard with determined finality as they tracked the dragon through the air above the village, Urick said, "This is for you, Orion," and jerked the lanyard.

The explosion was deafening.

The sheer force of the six charges igniting as one was enough to blow the cannon apart, the powerful concussion lifting Urick off his feet and sending him flying back through the air, spinning shards of hot iron from the demolished cannon hissing past all around him.

The harpoon was launched skyward, the gleaming point of Orion's dagger flashing sharply in the sunlight as it streaked across the sky like a comet.

Temper had made it out over the lake, his tattered, injured wings carrying him on an uneven flight as he attempted to flee the villagers' fierce mutiny. Just then the harpoon arched down out of the sky, ripping through his wing and punching deep into his exposed flank.

Releasing a blood-curdling roar of pain, Temper was folded in half by the harpoon's impact as he fell from the sky like a demon cast from the heavens. Then the monstrous, battered dragon crashed into the lake with a giant splash, the reporting spout of water shooting fifty feet into the air.

For several long moments all the shocked villagers gathered together could do was watch, wide eyed and unbelieving, as the giant circle of frothy water churned with bubbles, the huge waves radiating outward across the lake's surface.

They had done it...They'd killed Temper...

The villagers' collective cry of victory that followed could be heard for miles around.

## CHAPTER 32

"An' here's to that scaly bastard: May yeh rot in hell, yeh scurvy salamander!" Horris yelled joyously, raising his sloshing mug over his head.

The villagers crowded tightly into the pub cheered roisterously and raised their mugs as well, the celebration of Temper's death having just begun.

"Now take 'er down the hatch!" Horris said, knocking back his mug and guzzling the entire cup at once, the thick mead dribbling from the corners of his mouth and into the curly tangles of his beard.

Not needing any persuasion, the villagers followed Horris's lead. Men, women, the elderly, and even some children guzzled down the sour, potent alcohol in celebration of this joyful event. Temper, the plague which had for so many long years cast a dark cloud of fear all across the land, was now gone! Each and every one of them felt as though they'd awoken from a nightmare to a new, worry-free life stretching blessedly ahead of them-- They were free!

Horris lowered his mug, releasing a startlingly powerful belch, and wiped his thick forearm across his mouth before announcing, "Lastly, but most importantly, I say we thank Nethaneal. Who woulda thought such a pretty lad would have it in him to battle dragons, eh?" He spread his arms wide, and with a comical look of challenge, repeated in a booming voice, "'Go ahead, **mighty** Temper, take yer bes' shot!'"

The pub erupted into laughter, some doubling over and spraying ale from their nostrils at Horris's hilarious rendition of the duel. The fight had been so bloody, so unbelievably harrowing, that it felt wondeful to be able to laugh about it now.

"Pay the man his money!" a man called out from the rear of the uproarious crowd. "Yeah, he earned every round of it!" someone else agreed.

At the time of the Dragon Slayer's demands a hundred gold coins had seemed like a ridiculous bounty, absurd. But now, experiencing the blessed freedom they'd been deprived of while cowering under Temper's rule, the gold was suddenly insignificant in comparison--nothing.

Amid the collective, encouraging cheers of the increasingly intoxicated patrons, Horris reached under the bar and produced the large sack of coins he'd stored there for safe keeping.

"Truth be told, we're still in yer debt," Horris said with all sincerity, tossing the pouch into the air.

Standing across the cluttered pub with Maribel at his side, Nethaneal caught the sack of coins in one hand with a metallic jangle. His other arm was tightly wrapped in a white bandage and hung from a sling around his neck.

"Thank you, everyone, thank you!" Nethaneal said with a smile. As the cheers of the villagers died out he held up the heavy sack of gold coins, seeming to consider his hard-earned payment. But after a thoughtful moment Nethaneal's blue eyes softened as he scanned over the exuberant faces of the villagers watching him in expectant silence. His smile slowly faded.

"I don't think I can rightly accept this," Nethaneal announced, much to everyone's surprise. Before the murmurs could begin he continued on, "I would be dead right now, if it wasn't for all of you coming to my rescue...And in doing so several of you even sacrificed your lives. Perhaps it is I who should be indebted to you. Today, all of you are Dragon Slayers."

With that, Nethaneal tossed the sack of gold coins back across the pub to Horris, who caught it with a troubled look of puzzlement on his ruddy face. "We gotta show our gratitude somehow," he said, his bushy eyebrows pinching together with concern, "Jus' wouldn't be right."

Nethaneal put his good arm around Maribel's shoulders and smiled affectionately down at her. "I'm sure we can figure something out...right?" he asked, hugging her close.

Maribel smiled blushingly as the entire pub looked on in silence, glancing to her father for approval of the marriage.

Urick stood in the crowd nearby, several cuts from the exploding cannon's shrapnel marring his stern features. For a moment he said nothing, the villagers holding their breath in collective anticipation. Then, realizing he'd lost one son only to gain another, a smile crossed Urick's face as he said, "I would be honored."

"Now I can drink to that!" Horris roared, slamming an entire keg on the counter and ripping off its lid. "Come an' get it, lot--Tonight it's on the house!"

Lifting their mugs in a unified cheer of merriment, the villagers surged forward towards the bar, laughing and cursing joyfully.

The celebration of Temper's death and the union of Maribel and Nethaneal had not been long underway when the door of the pub suddenly swung open, revealing Conner standing in the doorway with a grin of snide anticipation on his pale, angular face.

Upon returning to the village Conner had expected to find the villagers mourning the death of their beloved "Dragon Slayer" and dreading the return of Temper's impending wrath. What he found, however, was quite the opposite: The villagers packed inside the pub were cheering and laughing, drinking ale and making merry in victorious celebration. A crowd of admirers was gathered around Nethaneal, and tucked at his side Maribel stood smiling lovingly up at him, one hand on his chest.

Conner's face slackened with horrified disbelief as he
realized that despite his best efforts to sabotage his weapon,
the Dragon Slayer must have still succeeded in killing Temper. If
this was the case, he'd never win Maribel back. Conner felt his
heart drop sickeningly into his stomach. This was the most
terrible thing he could have ever imagined.

And then it got even worse.

A burly man standing across the smoky pub suddenly pointed
directly at him and yelled above the clamorous sounds of the
celebration, "Ey! There's the filthy traitor--**GET HIM!**"

His beady eyes stretching wide with fear as he realized he'd
been found out, Conner let out a womanish scream of terror and
bolted out the door, a mob of angry, drunken men hot on his
heels.

Filling the pub, the villagers continued to **laugh** and
celebrate all the more.

CHAPTER 33

Meanwhile...

Temper's massive body sank into the lake's watery depths in
a gracefully lifeless descent, crimson tendrils of dark blood
leaking from his many wounds swirling gently all around him. Like
the last precious pearl of life, an air bubble escaped from
Temper's yawning mouth and shimmied upward, fleeing back towards
the surface.

Down, down into the water's depths the dragon's torn body
continued to descend. And as it did so the sun's glimmering rays
became an ever-distant memory as the darkening water enveloped
Temper's nightmarish corpse, sealing it away in its cold,
lifeless abyss.

After a long descent Temper's corpse came to a sluggish rest
on the lake bottom, a disturbed cloud of silt rising in a slow

plume all around his huge reptilian body. And it was there in its
watery grave that one would expect the dragon's corpse to stay,
becoming bloated and soft, his putrefying flesh picked over by
nibbling fish, until only his bones littered the lake bottom, a
horrid, distant memory sealed away in the depths of time.

But it didn't.

A strong, steady current which flowed along the lake's rocky
bottom rolled Temper's body over onto his side. Then one of the
dragon's tattered wings was gradually folded open by the force
of the shimmering water, and like a ship's sail being filled with
wind, Temper's wing began to drag his limp body, inch by inch,
along the lake floor.

Long neck, legs, and tail dragging through the disturbed
silt, Temper's body was gently pulled in the current to a steep
decline. There the dragon's body slid off the edge and tumbled
in a slow roll down the precipice and to the bottom of a steep
gorge. There the current increased in force and speed, carrying
the dragon's lifeless body into a massive underwater cavern from
which the current was being drawn. Here the current became a
roaring froth of water as it was funneled into the cavern and
rushed through the rocky subterranean passage, through erratic
twists and turns of stone worn smooth over eons.

Temper's limp body was carried on this frantic rush of water
like a monstrous piece of debri for some time, until finally the
narrow passageway opened up to a looming, subterranean cavern.
There the rapids were released out into a giant pool of black,

calming water. Temper's body floated across the surface of this
pool until his monstrous, torn and bloodied corpse finally washed
against a stone ledge. Here it stayed, the ink-black water
lapping around his body in the absolute darkness of the cavern,
unmoving and lifeless.

That is, until one of Temper's red eyes slid open.

PRESENT DAY


     Temper awoke into sheer darkness, laying curled on the cold,
hard stone floor of the subterranean cavern. His stomach churned
with hunger, telling him it was time to feed.

     Stiff from old age and his long slumber, the crippled dragon
struggled to his feet, now but a withered, haggard shell of his
once fearsome image. His formally deadly horns were now but
uneven stumps protruding from over his faded, tired red eyes.
Puckered scars marred his dull scales in webbed patches of pale
flesh on his face, chest, neck, and flanks. The imposing muscles
which had once bulged beneath his scales were now gone, his
flesh hanging loosely off his frame, his ribs and vertebrae now
visible. His wings, crippled and torn to rags, were tucked
uselessly at his sides.

     Finally getting to his feet, Temper slowly lumbered away

with his tail dragging behind him, revealing that he'd been
sleeping protectively on his bed of treasures: Several crumpled
beer and soda cans; a rusted license plate; a pair of metal
sunglasses with one lense shattered out; a half dozen fishing
lures; a yellow-handled screwdriver; and a cheap metal watch--
various shiny pieces of trash which had caught Temper's eye and
sufficed to remind him of the brilliant mountains of treasure
he'd once possessed.

Coming to the end of the stone ledge in the subterranean
cavern, Temper gingerly lowered his head and slipped into the
black pool of water, his scaled body disappearing beneath the
surface. Using the ever-increasing current of water to aid his
movements, Temper allowed himself to be pulled into one of the
tunnels through which the roaring surge of water flowed. Through
erratic twists and turns Temper was carried through the
underground network of waterways, using his long serpentine neck
to steer his way along the sunless maze he had memorized hundreds
of years ago. After some time Temper's monstrous body came
gliding out into yet another swirling pool of water where he
paused to raise his head above the surface and take in a breath,
mist bursting from his nostrils. Then he arched his neck and dove
beneath the surface once more, using his tail like a fin to
propel himself deeper and deeper into the tight stone confines of
the aquifer. After several long minutes of descent the ink-black
water suddenly exploded into a dazzling sea of sunlit green as
Temper emerged from the mouth of another submerged cavern and

into the fresh lake water.

Once out in open water, Temper unfolded his massive tattered wings and gave them a slow, surging beat. Although rendered incapable of flight, Temper's wings now served to propel him through the water, his legs tucked back, his tail flowing behind him as he gracefully navigated the rocky, silt-covered lake bottom.

Gliding through the water, Temper swept his head to the side and gnashed his teeth at a fleeing school fo salmon, consuming a third of them at once.

Navigating for a time through watery valleys and submerged peaks, Temper gave his wings a slow beat as he ascended upward for air. The dragon's head breached the lake's surface a moment later in a mass of churning bubbles, the sun's rays glittering off the disturbed ripples spreading all around him. Water running down his glistening head and long scaled neck, Temper's slitted pupils narrowed in the bright sunlit world, a world he had once ruled but now only dared to venture out into on the rarest of occasions.

Bordering the lake, rolling green mountains rose to the clear blue sky. The sun was shining brightly overhead, and far in the distance a speeding boat sent a tail of mist flying in its wake. Having seen the giant creature emerge from the water, a herd of deer which had been drinking at the shoreline quickly broke away and trotted into the trees.

Temper growled, angry that he'd missed the chance at a meal.

Knowing he couldn't risk staying above the surface for long lest
the humans spot him, Temper again arched his long neck and
slipped beneath the surface, the powerful surge of his beating
wings sending a surge of lapping waves across the lake's placid
surface as he departed.

The irony was not lost on Temper. He knew, bitterly, that
the humans had long come to reclaim the land, and that in his
condition there was no way he could ever hope to reestablish his
dominance over them. He also realized that if the humans had so
nearly managed to kill him, then they had surely slain every
other dragon in all the lands. He was alone in the world, Temper
knew, wounded, crippled, and forced into hiding, relegated to
eating wriggling fish and the occasional animal venturing too
close to the water's edge. For a dragon that had once held so
much power, so much land, and so much fear over the humans, it
was infuriating to admit that he now feared them enough to lead
such an ignominious, cowardly existence.

Temper was gliding through the water near the shallows as
this thought simmered in his mind, searching for meager fish or
turtles to snap up, when a blurry silhouette shimmering on the
lake's surface nearby suddenly caught his attention.

Instinctively folding in his crippled wings, Temper's
monstrous scaled body slowly settled down onto the rocky lake
bottom with a plume of silt. Sensing a meal, Temper then began to
stalk forward across the lake bottom, long neck coiled back,
ready to strike.

But as he neared the clear water shallows, the blurry
silhouette gradually defined itself: It was a human, standing
alone at the shore.

Feeling a long dormant bloodlust beginning to burn anew
in his core, Temper's slitted black pupils narrowed to a knife's
edge in his red eyes. His scaled lips peeled back from his dull
yellowed teeth as he began to growl, low and powerful, the heat
of his breath still enough to boil the water around his muzzle.

He might not be able to kill them all, Temper realized, but
maybe he could take one more, for old time's sake.

Longing for the taste of human flesh, the taste which had
for so long been denied him, Temper continued to stalk forward
into the shallows, a deadly presence lurking just below the
surface.

CHAPTER 35


The little blonde-haired boy stood ankle deep in the shallow water, pants rolled up to his knees, skipping rocks out across the glittering, sunlit water. Slip-p-p-p...Slip-p-p-p... Slip-p-p-p...Slip-p-p-p-p...

Running out of rocks, the boy bent down and began feeling for flat stones on the shore, squinting eagerly through the shallow, sparkling water at his feet.

Not just any rock would do. A good skipping rock had to be flat--but not too flat--with rounded edges like a pancake. It couldn't be too light or too heavy either, because a little heft ensured a good, long skip.

The boy had just managed to locate such a rock when suddenly several small waves appeared from out of nowhere on the lake's flat surface and came lapping onto shore around his ankles.

Curious, the boy straightened up and squinted out over the water, eyes tracking across the lake's smooth, glimmering surface for what had created such a disturbance.

Suddenly goosebumps appeared on his arms as a shiver went down his spine.

Something, the boy sensed at that moment, was out there.

The boy was still searching the lake for a passing boat, a gust of wind, anything which could explain the odd surge of water, when--

"Bobby? What are you doing down here?" a woman's voice asked.

Startled, Bobby flinched and turned around, dropping the skipping rock with a plop at his side. Finding his mother standing on the shore behind him, he smiled with relief and whispered excitedly, "I think Nessy's out there, mommy!"

The woman smiled lovingly from the bank, amused that her son believed that such a fanciful thing as the Loch Ness Monster could really exist. "You do?" she asked with mock amazement, putting her hands on her hips. "I have an idea: How about you come eat lunch, and then we'll look for Nessy together, okay?"

"Okay mommy!" the boy said, eagerly splashing out of the water to join his mother as they walked off hand in hand.

After they were gone, the surface of the lake ten yards out swelled, rippled ominously, and then went flat.